The Only Game In Town

The Only Game In Town

A Novel

Gordon Donnell

iUniverse, Inc.
New York Lincoln Shanghai

The Only Game In Town

iUniverse books may be ordered through booksellers or by contacting:

iUniverse
2021 Pine Lake Road, Suite 100
Lincoln, NE 68512
www.iuniverse.com
1-800-Authors (1-800-288-4677)

This is a work of fiction. All of the characters, names, incidents, organizations, and dialogue in this novel are either the products of the author's imagination or are used fictitiously.

ISBN-13: 978-0-595-43853-2 (pbk)
ISBN-13: 978-0-595-88178-9 (ebk)
ISBN-10: 0-595-43853-9 (pbk)
ISBN-10: 0-595-88178-5 (ebk)

Printed in the United States of America

1

The two men passed silently along the Elysian Hotel's 31ˢᵗ floor corridor. John Congo stopped just short of the executive suite. Clint Phillips planted his six feet seven inches and two hundred sixty pounds in front of the door. His growl barely disturbed the 1:00 AM stillness.

"Risking our butts to bust up a piss-ant crap game," he complained. "How smart is this?"

"Only the paranoid survive," Congo said.

Congo was a trim man in an expensive shawl-collar sweater, sharply creased woolen slacks and highly polished loafers. A man whose secrets were guarded by veneer. His eyes, behind the lenses of gold-rimmed spectacles, gave away nothing.

Phillips glanced at him uncertainly. "Are you sure that was the signal from Les?"

"I told him to blip the speed dial on his cell phone, cut the connection and ask to be let out."

"So that ring you got was either Les or a wrong—"

The latch clicked. Phillips raised his leg and drove his size twelve shoe against the door.

The door collided with something that absorbed most of the force of his kick. After that it continued inward in a lazy arc. A burly youth sat stunned on the carpet. Blood ran from his nose, covered his gaping mouth like smeared lipstick and dribbled from a slack jaw. Phillips stepped in and kicked him in the head. The youth slumped on the carpet and lay still.

In the suite, furniture had been pushed against the walls to make room for a crap table. Men crowded around in a haze of cigarette smoke. The addictive greed and fear that came with gambling had transported them to another world. Phillips had to whistle to get their attention.

"Cops," he warned. "Down in the lobby."

Most players snatched up wagers and scurried out. The unconscious doorman might have been a stain on the carpet for all the attention anyone paid to him.

A few players remained. Men who had come looking for action and would take it any way they could get it. A massive Polynesian with a spider tattooed on one cheek shuffled belligerently.

"They ain't no mu-fuckin' cops," he declared, and showed a gold tooth in a smile that dared someone to argue with him.

Phillips stepped past him to the table. It was a heavy casino model, banked and padded. Phillips squatted, wedged a shoulder under the frame and rose up like a power lifter. The table crashed over on its side. Phillips began kicking it, laughing with senseless glee when he split a seam in the playing surface.

Players eyed him nervously, backed away, and drifted out of the suite. Congo shut the door after the last of them.

Two men stood beside the ruined table. One was young and gangling, with a wispy goatee and hostile eyes. He still held the flimsy stick he had used to rake in lost bets and recover dice. The other man was thirty, dark-featured. He wore a sport coat cut to show off an athletic build.

"All right," he said, clamping a lid on the anger rising in his cheeks, "what's it all about?"

"Old bar cruising trick," Phillips explained with a touch of embarrassment in his grin. "If they think you're tough, they'll fight you. If they think you're a head case, they'll leave you alone."

"Yeah? And who's going to pay for—?"

Phillips stopped grinning and drove a huge fist into the man's midsection, doubling him over. Congo helped the man to an armchair and sat him down.

"My name's John Congo. What's yours?"

"Raymond Step—Stepanian," the man choked out.

"Do you prefer Raymond or Ray?"

"Raymond," he gasped. "Who the fuck are you guys?"

Congo sat in a companion chair. "I'm one of the owners of this hotel."

Stepanian gaped at him.

"You can imagine how upset I was," Congo went on, "when Phil called me at home and told me a waitress at a cocktail lounge tried to steer him to a dice game here."

Stepanian fidgeted. "It's no big worry. I barely break even."

"A four star hotel lives or dies by its reputation, Raymond. People come here from all over the world. They stay at the Elysian because they feel safe and well cared-for in a big, frightening foreign city. People bring their families here from all over the country. Decent, religious people. People who think gambling ought to be tucked away out of sight on Indian reservations."

"Like I was going to advertise."

"One sore loser could bring the police down on you, Raymond. And the news media down on the hotel. A little dice game is like a little cancer. It has to be cut out early."

"Okay." Stepanian held up his hands in a placating gesture. "I get the picture. I pick up my cash, you pay me for the layout your steroid wrecked, I'm gone. You never see me again."

The two chairs were set half facing each other, half facing the suite's main window. The drapes were open to the night. Los Angeles spread below, a lattice-work of pulsing lights, like the veins of some vast, slumbering creature. Congo stared out wordlessly.

Tiny beads of sweat appeared on Stepanian's upper lip. "You can't just throw me out on my ass. The sharks are into me, man. I owe major Benjamins."

"I hear Florida is nice this time of year."

"I got connections," Stepanian warned.

Congo raised his eyebrows. "The people who let you into the hotel?"

"You'll find out soon enough. Unless you think you can beat it out of me now."

"We're not thugs, Raymond."

"Yeah. Right." Stepanian came to his feet, testing his balance.

Phillips caught his lapel, said, "Come on, Ray, baby. I hear your elevator," and tugged Stepanian to the door.

The gangling stickman had roused the burly youth on the carpet but wasn't having any luck getting him to stand. Phillips caught the youth by the collar and hauled him to his feet. Raymond and the gangling stickman took the youth one under each arm. Phillips hustled them out.

Abe Lester came from the bedroom pulling a struggling woman by one arm. Taller than his five feet eight inches, bony and angular, she dressed to emphasize her height and managed an unlovely air of sophistication.

Congo ran his gaze up and down. "I didn't know there was any mileage left in the Jackie Kennedy look."

"Let me go or I scream rape."

"It's not my semen they'll scrape out of you."

Murder filled her eyes.

Lester had her wallet open in his free hand. "Rachel Lee Krebs," he read from a driver's license. He had the acerbic voice of an honest bookkeeper beset by sharpers. "Puts a pair of .32's in your back and whispers a hundred in your ear. Only you get to do the stick up."

"Up yours," she shrilled. "You ain't cops."

"Rachel," Congo began, but she cut him off.

"It's Lee. I hate Rachel."

"Fine. Just understand that this hotel isn't your business address."

"What did you do to Raymond?"

"Raymond is emigrating. You're welcome to join him."

She pulled free of Lester's grip, snatched her wallet and hurried out the door, almost colliding with a returning Clint Phillips.

"You should've let me pull Raymond's chain," the big man grumbled. "He would have talked. I know his type."

"He'd have lied," Congo said. "That's all his type knows."

"Christ, John, I haven't had any fun since you got this wild hair up your ass about going straight."

Congo stood, stripped off his shawl collar sweater and an armored vest beneath. Perspiration stained his shirt; silent witness to tension boiling within. He shivered in the machine-chilled air and put the sweater back on.

"Do me a favor, Phil. Take my vest down to the car. Pick us up out front. Les, you come with me. I want to talk to the manager about getting this mess cleaned up."

"Am I coming along to mediate?" Lester asked as they walked out to the elevator. "Or just administer first aid?"

Congo ignored the sarcasm and pushed the call button. "You played for half an hour, Les. What kind of operation was Raymond running?"

"Five and dime bustout. The table was bent. The dice were shaved. Half the players had an old lady on welfare."

"So how did a cheap operator like Raymond come to be working a four star hotel?"

"How did a cheap operator like you come to own a piece of a four star hotel?" Lester retorted.

Congo shot an irritable glance at him. "You know the story."

"All Phil and I know is what you spoon fed us. You bought a real estate company out of bankruptcy. Shares of stock in the hotel were part of the assets."

Congo said nothing.

The elevator door whispered open and they got on. The car was tastefully paneled in mahogany, barely perceptible in its descent. It put a hush into Lester's voice.

"Okay, John, keep your fucking secrets. I'm just the bean counter here. But I know there's more to it. They only let people like you into Federal court in handcuffs and leg irons."

"I paid," Congo insisted. "Straight up and legal."

The elevator let them out near the entrance to *Traders* restaurant, empty and dark at that hour. From there the nearly deserted lobby stretched most of a city block, past the Italian marble reception desk and the escalator that ran up to the Grand Ballroom, past the conversation area with its opulent sofas, to the discreet neon marking the cocktail lounge at the far end.

"Where's the manager's office?" Lester asked.

"Forget it," Congo said. "I see someone better."

Two men stood near the concierge desk, engrossed in conversation. They didn't resemble each other physically, but they were alike in more ways than they were different; large men made more so by executive luncheons; turned out in suits and accessories pricey enough to serve notice that they had risen to positions where their wishes prevailed and their shares would always be the greatest amounts. Congo strode over and extending his hand to the older man.

"Good morning, Mr. Hillman. My name is John Congo. I'm the new owner of Crestline Properties."

"Are you indeed?"

Even at sixty, Hillman's voice still had an aloof touch of eastern prep school. He took Congo's measure while they shook hands, sizing him up with small eyes guarded by pads of fat. Congo met the scrutiny with a bland smile.

"May I present my associate, Abraham Lester? Les, this is A. Royce Hillman. Chairman of the real estate management company that handles the hotel. His picture was in the newsletter we got last week."

For a moment Hillman was bathed in an aura of brilliance but it was only headlights shining through the glass of the nearby main doors as a late airport shuttle swung into the forecourt outside.

"Gentlemen, my chief executive officer, Pat Easter."

Florid and fifty, Easter stepped forward with a ready smile and an energetic handclasp. "Will you be staying with us tonight?"

"Actually," Congo said, "we happened on a dice game in the executive suite."

Hillman and Easter exchanged alarmed glances.

"We persuaded the operator to leave," Congo assured them, "but he did abandon a—"

"Persuaded?" Hillman interrupted.

"He left a dice table behind," Congo said as the main door opened and business travelers straggled in from the airport shuttle. "I'd like to have it removed as quickly and as quietly as possible."

A commotion arose among the arriving travelers. The crowd parted. Raymond Stepanian stood in the doorway. He was a ghastly shadow of the insolent hoodlum Clint Phillips had hustled out of the executive suite. He took a wavering step and couldn't take another. His eyes lost focus. Muscle tension evaporated. Gravity took him straight down until the elements of his body could no longer compress upon themselves. He pitched forward and landed face-first in a limp mass.

Easter snapped, "Nine One One!" at the concierge and turned his attention to the arriving guests. He urged them toward the registration desk with the polite persistence of a teacher herding first graders.

Congo used a loafer to nudge a blunt chrome revolver away from Stepanian's hand. Recent firing had stained the muzzle. The back of Stepanian's sport coat was sodden and scarlet. Before Congo could drop to one knee for a closer look, Lester caught his arm and spoke quietly in his ear.

"Nothing we can do for him, John. Time to eighty-six ourselves out of this play, huh?"

Congo pulled his arm free, shot a glance at Lester.

"Come on, John," Lester said. "What's the point of the owners paying the Hillman people to manage the hotel if you won't let them do their job?"

Hillman nodded sagely. "That might be best."

"We need to talk about this situation," Congo insisted.

"Do you play golf?" Hillman inquired.

"Where and when?"

"Los Angeles Country Club. Shall we say ten tomorrow morning?"

"Fine."

Sirens were howling through the night when Congo and Abe Lester climbed into Clint Phillips' Cadillac. Phillips pulled out of the Elysian's forecourt into sparse traffic.

"How'd it go?"

"Pop quiz," Congo said. "A cheap gambler and his two henchmen rough up a dice operator. Who will the police suspect when the operator turns up with a bullet in him?"

A red light jolted Phillips back to his driving. He brought the Cadillac to a tire-squealing stop.

"Raymond was shot?"

"We didn't stick around to get a medical opinion, but it looked that way to me. How about you, Les?"

"Whatever it was, we're in the clear. They'll find someone else's fingerprints or DNA or whatever."

"Eighty percent of all murder convictions are obtained on circumstantial evidence," Congo said.

"Where did you get that?"

"From the lawyer I hired when I had to shoot that ex-con who came after me in Portland."

"So what are the circumstances?"

"Judging from the timing, Raymond must have been shot while we were still upstairs. He made his way back into the hotel to get help."

"Then we got no alibis but each other," Lester said.

Silence filled the Cadillac.

2

The north course of the Los Angeles Country Club meandered among the canyons off Wilshire Boulevard, hidden from prying eyes by gnarled greenery. Its real estate value was astronomical, its status beyond price. No actor had ever been considered for membership. Even Royce Hillman could finagle no more than a back nine on short notice.

Hillman teed up, waggled an over-sized titanium driver above his ball and swung the club as if power were all that mattered. Pat Easter followed, attacking his shot with signature enthusiasm. Congo hit off with a smooth stroke and hoisted his bag to his shoulder. Hillman and Easter boarded an electric golf cart.

Fairway shots took them to a challenging green. Only Congo salvaged par. Easter replaced the flag stick.

"Nicely played, John. Do you mind if I call you John?"

"I don't even mind discussing last night's incident at the hotel," Congo said as they left the green.

Easter walked close enough to make his energy as oppressive as the cologne he sweated. "I have to ask, John, why you didn't report the matter to Royce or myself?"

Hillman flanked Congo on the other side. "Pat and I are there for you. We're only a phone call away."

"The operator moved a twelve foot dice table past your security," Congo reminded them.

"I've already spoken to the contractor," Hillman assured him.

"If the operator borrowed from loan sharks to buy that layout," Congo persisted, "his collateral was his life. He wouldn't risk that unless someone in authority guaranteed his safety."

A scowl drew Hillman's small features close together, like craters on a fleshy moon. "You seem well versed in the economics of illegal dice games."

"I have my own page in the Nevada Black Book," Congo said.

The two executives exchanged confused glances.

"The Nevada Gaming Commission," Congo explained, "keeps a file listing everyone permanently barred from owning, working or playing in any casino in the state."

Hillman and Easter boarded their golf cart without another word. The next hole was a long par three.

"Two hundred forty four yards," Hillman announced. "Fifty dollars says I can put a ball pin high."

Easter winked at Congo. "John's the gambler here."

"I live by the laws of probability," Congo said. "I'd no more bet on a golf shot than I would burn money."

They hit off and Hillman walked along the fairway with Congo. "Let's get past this dice game, John. What's your real concern about the Elysian Hotel? You got your shares almost accidentally, didn't you? When you bought Crestline Properties out of bankruptcy?"

"Beside forty five shares in the Elysian," Congo said, "I got a ten story office building with spot vacancies on six floors, a shopping center with one of the anchor storefronts empty and three apartment buildings that I can't bring to full occupancy until a court lets me evict the problem renters. Dividends from the hotel are keeping the company afloat while I turn the rental property around."

They caught up with Easter and the cart at the green. "Pat," Hillman asked, "do you suppose Karen Steele could help John lease up Crestline's commercial properties?"

"Why, yes. I'm sure she could."

"Why don't you see if you can set up a meeting?"

Easter used his cell phone as he rolled up the next fairway. Even his telephone manner was animated. He drove to where Congo was lining up his approach shot.

"Good news, John. Karen is excited about the Crestline account. She'll meet us at the clubhouse after we finish our nine holes."

◆　　　◆　　　◆

The ante-bellum clubhouse offered a terrace where sociable little cliques convened at umbrella tables. A stunning brunette sat alone, talking on a hands-free cell phone while she moved quick fingers over the keyboard of a laptop computer. She caught sight of Hillman and brought the call to a hasty conclusion. Closing the laptop, she stood slim and erect in a skirt tailored to emphasize long legs.

"Royce! Good morning!" An effervescent smile made her thirty-some years seem less.

Hillman presented her to Congo as Karen Steele and they all sat down. A few minutes of small talk revealed that she was a single mother who juggled raising two boys and a position with a prestigious Los Angeles real estate brokerage. Hillman and Easter excused themselves to return to work and left her alone with Congo.

"So," she said after a glance to make sure her cell phone screen was clear, "you're the man who outbid Royce for Crestline."

Surprise arched Congo's eyebrows. "Isn't Crestline a bit small for Hillman?"

"Word on the street is that he wants controlling interest in the Elysian Hotel."

"Crestline holds forty five shares out of nine hundred forty one," Congo said. "Not exactly a majority."

"Control doesn't always require majority ownership." She sipped iced tea while her eyes chided him for his lack of imagination.

"Does Hillman expect me to vote the Crestline shares his way if you can fill the commercial vacancies?"

"I would like to help." Her smile was hopeful.

"What will you need from me?"

She set her tea aside and opened the laptop. He answered a series of rapid-fire questions to give her a flavor of the property; interrupted at random whenever she had to type a quick response to an incoming e-mail. She requested a diagram of the shopping center; floor layouts and a stacking plan for the office building. They should show which spaces were vacant, which were occupied, rental rates, termination dates, any options to expand or renew existing leases. He scribbled her requirements on the back of a scorecard and tucked it into his pocket.

"Where can I call you when I have everything together?"

She gave him a business card. "Can I walk you to the parking lot?"

Lunch hour had filled the asphalt with sleek new luxury vehicles. Congo set his clubs down at the trunk of a 1960 Valiant. A small car in its day, it seemed large now. Sculptured lines left it hopelessly outdated in contrast with surrounding vehicles. Glistening black paint and cat's eye taillights gave it a vaguely sinister look. Karen inspected it uncertainly.

"Are you a collector?"

"It's an acquired taste," he admitted.

"How do you acquire a taste for something like this?"

"My mother was a carnival stripper. When she needed the trailer to entertain, I slept in the Valiant."

His voice had no more feeling than scar tissue. Karen's nervous smile was a wordless apology for her flippant intrusion into his personal life. He shrugged it off.

"I'll call you when I have the drawings ready."

"Yes, do." She touched his arm. "I want to hear from you."

He watched her cross to an immaculate white Lexus, checking the screen of her cell phone for messages she had missed while they were talking.

"Sucker," he scolded himself, but he grinned anyway.

The Valiant started instantly and ran without sound. Heat accumulated during a morning in the sun dissipated slowly in the snarl of noon traffic. Congo drove to his home in Los Feliz, in the green hills below Silver Lake Reservoir.

Movie people had come long ago, those who could not quite afford Beverly Hills, and built as lavishly as their means allowed. The people faded into the footnotes of history, but the flamboyant homes remained. Congo's was tropical art deco, white stucco with pastel accents. Noiseless pushbuttons controlled the interior lights. Solid construction smothered his footfalls in ghostly silence.

Showered and dressed in a business suit, Congo left in his workday transportation, a Boxster Porsche. Twenty minutes in traffic brought him to Crestline's aging office building. He bought a late takeout lunch from the ground floor Teriyaki restaurant, scowled at the slow elevator response in the lobby and rode to his suite on four.

"Hi, Muffie. Where's Mr. Phillips?"

The receptionist was a Chinese-American with an infectious smile. Childhood playmates had long since contracted her name from Mei Feng. She had come with Crestline Properties.

"He had to go to the Coronado Apartments. The police got called again. About that guy selling drugs."

"Did he talk to the elevator service people?"

"Twice."

Congo raided Phillips' paper-strewn cubicle for a roll of plans and carried them into his private office. The room was no larger than it needed to be to hold a refinished desk and two facing chairs. Artwork was limited to a weather-beaten carnival poster pressed flat in a glass frame and a line drawing of the old twin-engine airplane Congo maintained as a hobby. Abe Lester appeared at the door.

"How was the golf game, John?"

"Hillman isn't satisfied with managing the Elysian. He wants to control it."

"Did you pick another fight with him?"

"There's plenty of time for that later."

"You didn't park the Valiant in their fancy lot to let the rich boys know they were talking to carnival trash?"

"Always deal your cards face up," Congo said. "That forces people to either accept you or walk away. You can't be blindsided later."

"You ought to write down these philosophical gems. You've probably got a self-help book in you."

Congo ignored the sarcasm. "Hillman introduced me to a broker from one of the downtown offices. Someone with the connections to find decent tenants for the building and the shopping center."

"Get real, John. That kind of talent won't look twice at Crestline. Too small, too old, not enough commission. Who is this guy, anyway?"

"Karen Steele."

Alarm filled Lester's eyes. He glanced out at Muffie and closed the door.

"Jesus fucking Christ, John. The woman they call Flamingo?"

"She has the looks to back up the name."

"And a client list to die for. If this Hillman character sicced her on you, he's up to something. Ten to one he wants to keep you busy peeking up her skirt while he palms a shaver into the game."

"I'm counting on it," Congo said.

Lester looked as worried as he did confused.

"If Hillman thinks he has me contained," Congo explained, "he'll make his move. I'll be watching."

"Look, John," Lester began nervously, "normally I wouldn't bring this up, and I hope you don't take it wrong, but you've read enough psychology to know you're not playing with a full deck. Are you sure it's a good idea to take on any more stress. I mean, if things don't go right …"

Congo let his gaze wander to the city beyond his window. "Ever since I was a runny-nosed kid being dragged around the carnival circuit, I've ached for a place to call my own."

"So you've told me. More than once."

"I'm not getting any younger. Either I make my move or I kiss off the dream."

Lester smiled sadly. "John, you're not old money. You're not executive timber. You're not some hip young smart-ass with a shitload of stock options. You're a drifter. A loner. A cheap gambler who had a run of luck. You just don't fit."

"Which means that for me, Crestline is the only game in town," Congo said. "I intend to make it work."

Lester stood and left without further argument. A few minutes later he could be heard telling Muffie he would be gone the rest of the day.

Congo booted up his desk computer and brought up a spreadsheet while he ate. He unrolled the plans on his desk and spent the afternoon carefully penciling the information Karen Steele had requested into the nineteen spaces on the shopping center schematic and the ten floors of the office Building. It was nearly five when Muffie buzzed his line.

"Mr. Congo, Rachel Krebs is here to see you."

"Who?"

"Rachel Krebs. She says she met you at the Elysian Hotel last night."

Congo snapped his fingers.

"Show her in, please, Muffie," he said, and stood to greet his visitor.

Rachel Lee Krebs had changed almost beyond recognition. Her height and a baggy sweater worn unbuttoned over a print dress left her gaunt where last night she had seemed sleek. A shapeless denim bag hung from one shoulder. Rimless glasses emphasized an absence of make-up. A mousy smile apologized for the eyes that would not quite meet Congo's.

"Thank you for seeing me," she said in a barely audible voice.

Muffie interrupted briefly. "Mr. Congo, I'll be leaving now, if it's okay. I've got computer class tonight."

"That's fine, Muffie. Thank you."

Muffie closed the door, shutting Congo and Rachel Lee Krebs into his office.

"Please sit down, Lee."

"It's Rachel. I hate Lee." Her voice was low and bitter.

"I'm sorry. Rachel."

She sat down primly and set the denim bag carefully on her lap. Congo sat down and gave her a reassuring smile.

"I'm glad you stopped by, Rachel. I'm trying to understand what happened last night. I hope you can help me."

"Understand?" Her confusion flickered only briefly at the sound of Muffie's departure from the outer office.

"Who arranged for Raymond to operate the dice game in the Elysian Hotel?"

"Mr. Congo, I thought about this and thought about it," she said, reaching into her bag, "and I really don't want to do it but I don't know anything else I can do."

She took out a blue steel .22 target pistol, set the bag on the floor and stood. Putting one hand under the other to steady her aim, she leveled the long barrel at Congo's head.

3

Beads of sweat appeared on Congo's face. The distant echo of an air conditioning fan was the loudest sound in the room. Chilled air drifted from a ceiling vent. Congo shivered. He forced a smile and looked past the blue steel automatic to make eye contact with Rachel.

"I didn't kill Raymond," he assured her.

"He just wanted to be in the big time." She sniffled.

"You saw me in the hotel suite after he left," he reminded her.

"No!" She jerked her head from side to side.

"You talked to me in the hotel suite."

"It was Lee!" she shrilled.

"Rachel, try to remember—"

"Lee was there! Not me!"

The automatic twitched from the tension in her grip. Congo moistened his lips.

"You're right. It was Lee. I remember now. She told me her name."

The pistol steadied. "You ruined Raymond's dice game."

"Why did Raymond pick the Elysian, Rachel? Out of all the hotels in Los Angeles, why the Elysian?"

"Lee told him about it." She spat the words at Congo, as if she were voiding her mouth of a foul taste.

"How did Lee know about the Elysian, Rachel?"

"She just did. That's all."

"Does she work at the hotel?"

"Lee doesn't work. She never works."

"Where do you work, Rachel?"

"At Hillman Management." Pride squared her gaunt shoulders. "I'm the accounts payable bookkeeper."

Inspiration sizzled in the depths of Congo's eyes, like some fragment of tawdry neon. He settled back in his chair.

"You know, Rachel, of all the things I've done in my life, bookkeeping is the one I enjoyed most."

She blinked in surprise.

"I felt secure," he said. "Everything had a place, and I always knew where to put it."

She nodded agreement.

"That's all I was trying to do last night," he said. "Trying to put things in their right place. You know Raymond didn't belong in the Elysian, don't you, Rachel?"

She squirmed, said nothing.

"Not even if Royce Hillman let the dice game into the hotel," he said.

"Lee is the one he talks to," Rachel insisted. "Mr. Hillman. Lee is the one who does those awful things with him."

"Does Hillman bully the people who work for him?"

Rachel just stared.

"Does he threaten to fire them if they don't do what he wants?" Congo asked.

"He fired six people today."

"Is that why you came, Rachel? Is that why you're angry?"

She shook her head in a tight, tense arc. "Not me. Six other people."

Surprise etched a frown into Congo's features. "Did he say why?"

"It was a reorganization, so the company could be more competitive." She bit her lip. "He even fired Mr. Byner."

"Who?"

"Ewald Byner. He was my supervisor. He worked there for twenty three years. It just wasn't fair."

"Do you feel vulnerable?" Congo asked. "Because your supervisor was fired?"

"I'm not going to kill you."

She took her free hand from under the pistol, stooped and hefted her denim bag. Still pointing the automatic at Congo's head, she backed toward the door.

"I decided."

"Thank you, Rachel."

"Don't do that!" she shrilled. "Don't be polite. I decided. Me. It hasn't got anything to do with you."

Her bag was clumsy and she had to set it down to open the door. She retrieved the bag and retreated into the reception area. Wary eyes warned against following her. Congo smiled and sat perfectly still.

The outer door made noise opening and closing. Congo's fingers trembled as he used a handkerchief to pat the dampness from his face. He went out to the reception area and locked the outer door.

The telephone books behind the reception counter listed only one Ewald Byner. Congo's call lasted no longer that it took to establish that Byner was at home and would be for the rest of the evening. A book of spiral bound maps guided Congo out Topanga Canyon Boulevard and into a moderately affluent section of the San Fernando Valley. The address he had copied was on a street of well-kept older tract homes. A man was absorbed in washing a sedan in the driveway. Congo parked and walked as close as he could without being sprayed.

"Mr. Byner?"

Byner was the size and shape of a bear. He lumbered to the house, shut off the hose and came back, wiping large hands on shapeless khaki trousers. A sweatshirt and a walrus mustache completed his rumpled look.

"Are you the one who called?"

"My name is John Congo, Mr. Byner. I apologize for intruding on your evening."

Byner extended a damp paw. "I hope you haven't had a trip for nothing. You hung up before I gathered the presence of mind to explain my situation."

"Is there someplace we can talk?"

Byner led Congo through a carport with garden tools hung on the back wall. A door let them into a cheerful kitchen. Signs of hectic family life ranged from a refrigerator door crammed with magnet notes to a sink full of dishes. Rock music came muffled from the depths of the house. Congo declined coffee but accepted a seat at the Formica table. Byner sagged into a chair across from him.

"I'm sorry if I seem a little scattered. I had twenty odd years of my life ripped away today. All I could think to do was wash the car."

"Did you have any notice?" Congo inquired.

Byner eyed him closely. "I'm not sure I understand your interest?"

"I own Crestline Properties."

"Staffing changes wouldn't affect Hillman's contract to manage the Elysian Hotel."

"When the management firm is reorganized without notice, it makes me nervous," Congo said. "I'd appreciate any insight you could provide."

"My severance agreement includes non-disclosure and non-disparagement clauses," Byner informed him. "The money involved isn't lavish, but I have three children to put through college."

"What was your position at Hillman? That should be public knowledge."

"Controller." Byner's uncompromising stare suggested confidentiality went beyond his severance agreement to issues of personal integrity.

"The value of the Elysian is public knowledge also," Congo pushed on. "One hundred thirty million dollars on the tax rolls. Deducting sixty million for the mortgage leaves seventy million in equity. It would cost thirty five million plus to by a majority interest."

"What do you want, Mr. Congo?" Byner asked in a level rumble. "I mean behind the smile and the glib talk, what do you really want?"

"I just want my cards off the top of the deck. I don't think that's too much to ask."

"That's not an answer."

"Thirty five million is a lot of money," Congo said. "Let's assume Hillman doesn't have it, or doesn't want to put it at risk if he does. Does he have means of gaining control other than buying a majority interest?"

"You're talking to the wrong man," Byner said. "I wasn't invited to any of the meetings Royce and Pat held with the consultants and lawyers."

"Did they ask you to look over any numbers?"

That drew a rueful smile from Byner. "My wife tells me I missed a clue there. I should have seen the axe swinging."

"How is she taking this?"

Byner's hair was thinning and the anger that colored his face was visible up into his scalp. "What's that about? A little phony sympathy to make me think you care?"

Congo raised a placating hand. "Okay, it's none of—"

"I've handled money all my adult life. I've had to talk to my share of con men over the years. You all think you're so damned slick, don't you?"

Congo lowered his hand. His smile was properly chastened. He allowed a moment to pass in silence before he spoke again.

"Did you know the man who was killed at the Elysian last night?"

"Why do you ask?"

"I'm not trying to implicate you," Congo assured him. "I'm just curious if you know anything about his relationship with Rachel Krebs."

Byner said nothing, waiting with wise eyes for Congo to commit himself to more specific questions.

"As controller," Congo said, "an obvious sleaze romancing the woman who wrote your company's checks had to cause you some concern."

"Rachel has a moral compass," Byner said. "I wonder if you do."

"I'm sorry if I haven't made the best impression," Congo said.

"You've imposed on my grief looking for information you have no right to," Byner said. "You pry into my personal life. You impugn Rachel's integrity. You don't seem to give a damn about anyone but yourself."

"We both know Rachel isn't the most stable individual," Congo persisted. "How bad is it? I mean, what is she capable of?"

Byner dismissed the idea with a snort. "Royce has industrial psychologists in on a regular basis. Active listening. Proactive thinking. Habits of success. The criticism sessions are brutal. Any serious problems would have surfaced."

"Hillman enjoys bullying people?"

"Royce didn't invent management by psychobabble."

"Does he enjoy harassing female employees?"

"If any of the reputed hush money was actually paid, it didn't go through the company books. At least not while I was controller."

"I'm not suggesting you're involved in anything," Congo said. "I'm just trying to get a fix on whom and what I'm dealing with."

"All with a nice smile," Byner observed.

"I can frown, if you'd prefer," Congo said.

"No real emotion," Byner said. "How about a sense of right and wrong? Do you know the difference, or do you just make an educated guess based on experience and the behavior of people around you?"

"Mr. Byner, I didn't come here to—."

Byner stood, looming and hulking. "I think you're a damned psychopath. I want you out of my home. Right now."

Congo shrugged to lighten his disappointment. "Thank you for your time," he said and stood. "As far as your severance agreement is concerned, we never talked."

On the way home Congo pressed Clint Phillips' number into his cell phone.

"Yeah?" A bleary growl with TV noise in the background.

"Pick me up as soon as you can," Congo instructed. "We're going hunting."

"You're going hunting. I was up until two thirty this morning."

"You can sleep tomorrow night."

"Christ, John, what's got your spankies in a knot this time?"

"Hillman sacked his head of accounting today. That happens for one of two reasons. Either the guy was breaking the rules, or he wasn't giving the other executives a chance to. This guy didn't strike me as a crook."

"Well, you're the expert on crooks, but what the hell are you going to do about it?"

"We need to locate Raymond's two friends. I think there was a lot more to last night's dice game than meets the eye."

4

"You got any bright ideas how we find these two bad boys?" Phillips asked when he had his Cadillac rolling.

"Let's start with the waitress who steered you to the game," Congo said.

"What the hell would she know?"

"Let's find her and ask her."

Phillips lapsed into uncomfortable silence. What he had told Congo was a cocktail lounge turned out to be an exotic dance club under the take-off pattern of LAX; a windowless building fronted by an asphalt parking strip. Sultry music assaulted them when they pushed in, loud enough to smother the jet noise and numb the senses. Most of the light was focused on a small stage. A woman strutted between two brass poles, working them into a limber stretch and pose number polished to a professional rote. Sweat glistened like rhinestones on her bare skin. Congo thrust the cover charge at a bored heavyweight and shot a glance at Phillips.

"How did you find this high class establishment?"

"I just came in for a look," the big man mumbled. "The sign said it was amateur night. All the babes had to be over six feet tall to compete."

"Where's your waitress."

Phillips squirmed. "Look, John, I know your mother—"

"Let's don't talk about it."

"Well, all right, damnit. Sulk if you want." Phillips led the way to an empty table and nodded when the waitress arrived.

"What are you drinking?" she asked.

Congo held up a twenty dollar bill. "You steered my friend to a dice game last night."

Her smile vanished.

"This isn't trouble," Congo assured her. "I just want to talk to the two men who were with Raymond."

"I don't know any Raymond." A skin hue close to Stepanian's suggested otherwise.

"Twenty if you pass the message along. Twenty more if you can get them to come here. The drinks are on me."

She took the money. "You better give me your orders. The management doesn't like dry tables."

She crossed to a phone beside the bar, spent five minutes in unheard conversation then returned with a pitcher of beer and two glasses.

"They won't come here," she said and wrote a telephone number on a coaster. "Wait twenty minutes and call. They'll tell you where."

Congo paid her and she moved off immediately.

Phillips filled the glasses and drained half his own at a single pass. Heavy jets departing overhead sent ripples shuddering across the surface of the beer in the pitcher. The dancer left the stage to tepid applause and scattered profanity. The music changed to a quicker beat. The lights shifted to a combination runway and bar where most of the sparse crowd sat. A young Asian woman in a satin bikini bottom strutted and gyrated from man to man, giving each a chance to tuck folding money inside her elastic, working them like human ATMs. Two more dancers plied their trade before Congo took out his cell phone and called the number from the coaster.

"Yeah?" The voice was masculine, young and taunting.

"My name is John Congo. Who am I speaking with?"

"You ain't speaking. You're just listening. You got that?"

"No one is looking for trouble," Congo said pleasantly. "Why don't you stop by for a drink? I'm buying."

"You know the Eldorado Motel in Anaheim?"

"No. I don't."

"Then you better look it up. You got forty five minutes to get there. Room three seventeen. Forty five minutes, or we're gone. Move your ass."

Dead air followed. Congo put the phone away. Phillips drained Congo's glass to fortify himself.

"Okay," he said, wiping his mouth with the back of his hand. "Where do we go?"

"A third floor room in a two story motel in Anaheim."

"You think it's a set-up?"

"Ten to one they're waiting outside to follow us until we're on a lonely stretch of road."

Anger darkened Phillips' face. "Damnit, John, you sat there twenty fucking minutes knowing this was going to happen."

"It's the quickest way to make contact."

"We could get blown away over a lousy crap game."

"You never learn, do you, Phil?"

"What's that supposed to mean?"

"Remember your one glorious year in the NFL? You should. You've told me about it often enough. Train hard, give it everything on game day and don't worry about a little pain in that knee. Well, if you don't catch trouble when it's small, it grows up and eats you."

"A bum knee is just the breaks."

"Is that what you told Eileen? Before you found out that love, honor and obey only lasted as long as the money kept coming?"

"Back off, John." Phillips' voice was low and savage.

"All right. Give me the keys. You can catch a cab."

"This is fucking crazy."

Congo made a face. "I'd like to meet just one person who didn't think I was nuts."

"What did they call it in the Nevada Black Book?" Phillips asked. "Brief reactive psychosis?"

"That's from sore losers," Congo said.

"No, it's a fancy way of saying you bottle your problems up inside until they boil out under the lid."

Congo held out his hand for the keys.

Resistance leaked out of Phillips in a hopeless sigh. "Well, shit, let's get it over with, then."

The thunder of a departing jet greeted them as they pushed out the front door. Dusk had faded into night. Traffic on Imperial was a rolling stream of lights that turned parked cars into silhouettes and cast creeping shadows. Congo and Phillips took separate routes to the Cadillac so they couldn't both be hit by a single burst of gunfire.

Phillips got in and opened the passenger door for Congo. "Well, so far, so good."

Congo buckled himself in. "Head east on Imperial. If we're not followed, we'll have to find a phone booth and look up that motel."

Phillips merged into traffic, dividing his attention among other cars, the Cadillac's mirrors and his thoughts.

"Eileen put up with a lot from me. I'm not sure we would have lasted even if my knee hadn't taken me out of the pros."

"Forget it. I was out of line bringing it up."

"If I just had another chance with her, maybe I could"—Phillips' eyes locked on the side mirror—"I don't fucking believe this."

"What?"

"If you were following someone, trying to be innocuously inconspicuous and all that shit, would you be driving a fire-engine red Trans-Am?"

Congo didn't look. "How many in the car?"

"Two."

"Keep your eyes open. The Trans-Am may just be flash. Something to distract us from the real shooters."

"I don't think so, John. They look like the hormones we threw out of the hotel."

Eastbound traffic took the Cadillac through Hawthorne in fitful bursts, one stoplight to the next. They passed under the Harbor Freeway. Tall intersection lamps spread sodium light over the decay of Watts. Industrial buildings rose darkly in the background as they approached Alameda.

"Turn south," Congo instructed.

"Do you know what they do to white boys they catch in Compton after dark?"

"What kind of television have you been watching?"

"The Eleven O'clock News."

Flanked by dim factories and warehouses, Alameda was a thoroughfare for massive eighteen wheelers that rumbled to and from the Harbor at San Pedro. Dwarfing the trucks, a forlorn shunt of railroad cars waited on embedded iron rails.

"Make a U-turn around those freight cars," Congo ordered. "Kill the lights and find someplace to hide."

Phillips reacted with tire-squealing urgency. An air horn blasted as he cut in front of a semi. Ragged paving made a narrow passage between the railroad cars and the dark mass of a warehouse. He switched off his lights and accelerated. Passing headlight beams flickered beneath and between the freight cars. A hooded lamp showed an open gate in the fence beyond the warehouse. Phillips braked to a sliding stop, slammed the Cadillac into reverse and backed down the length of a loading dock, guided by the glow from tall doors open to serve parked semi trailers. He hid behind a dark tractor unit parked at the end.

Another air horn sounded out on Alameda.

Phillips cracked his door. "The flak jackets are in the trunk. So's my twelve gauge."

"Forget it. They saw the vests last night. They'll have something with enough velocity to penetrate. And they're no good to us dead."

"We're no good to us dead, either," Phillips grumbled, but he shut the door.

Shadows began to crawl in the warehouse yard, set in motion by slow moving lights out on the margin of Alameda. A brilliant halogen beam knifed the length of the yard. Hidden behind the tractor unit, Congo and Phillips could not see the source any more than they could be seen by those wielding the beam.

"Fucking amateurs," Phillips growled. "Lighting themselves up like cops. What are they going to pull next?"

"Nothing here. Not with a night crew in the warehouse."

The halogen beam was gone as quickly as it had come.

"Easy now," Congo said. "We don't want to tip them we're behind them."

"You want to follow these jokers?"

"Right now we've got them where we want them. If they pop out of the wood-work next week, it might be the other way around."

Phillips idled along to the end of the loading dock with his lights out, drifting to a stop so he would show no brake lamps. Visible a scant hundred yards away along the margin of Alameda were the running lights of the Trans-Am. They were not moving. The two men in the car were animated silhouettes in the lights of passing traffic.

"They're talking it over," Phillips decided. "We're dog food if they double back."

Minutes lingered, anxious and furtive, as if time itself was afraid to move. Finally the Trans-Am began rolling along the margin of Alameda, gathering speed until it could merge into traffic.

"Don't lose them," Congo said.

Phillips gave the Trans-Am plenty of distance on Alameda and then more when they turned west on Slauson. The final turn was onto a quiet street of mod-est homes. The Trans-Am pulled into a driveway. Its lights went out. Phillips cut his own lights and pulled to the curb half a block back. He shut off the engine.

Congo shouldered his door open. "Let's catch those clowns before they get inside."

Phillips had to move quickly to keep up. The two youths were already out of the Trans-Am. A street light above illuminated them and blinded them to the night around. The gangling stickman from the dice game opened the rear hatch.

"What a fucking waste. You and your big fucking let's go get them."

The burly youth who had guarded the door to the game took a soft-sided rifle case from the car. "Those fuckers whacked Uncle Ray." A bandaged nose forced him to breath audibly through his mouth. "Uncle Ray was cool, and I don't for-get who—"

"Gentlemen, may I have a word with you?"

Absorbed in their own squabble, the two had no warning of Congo's approach. Phillips snatched the rifle case from the startled doorman and grinned, daring him to retaliate.

Congo put himself in front of the gangling youth.

"We just want to talk, but if you want more, we can accommodate you."

The youth fidgeted, said nothing.

"What's your name?" Congo asked.

"Anton. Tony."

"What about him?" Congo glanced at the doorman.

"That's Nicky."

"He called Stepanian Uncle Ray. Are you brothers?"

"Cousins."

"Which of you is going to tell me who arranged for your uncle to operate in the Elysian Hotel?"

The two youths exchanged surprised glances.

"How would we know?" Tony asked.

"Uncle Ray didn't tell us those details," Nicky said in the voice that had taunted Congo on the telephone.

"All right, then, tell me when Raymond moved the game into the hotel. You must know that."

"Sunday," Nicky said defiantly.

"You were there only four days?"

"We hardly got going when you busted things up."

"After the game broke up, all three of you got into an elevator together. Where did you get off?"

"On the moon," Nicky said.

Phillips shoved the youth and sent him stumbling against the Trans Am.

Tony spoke up quickly. "In the lobby. We went out front and Uncle Ray put Nicky and me in a cab. Nicky, he wasn't feeling so good."

"Did your uncle say where he was going?"

Tony shook his head.

Nicky sneered. "He went after you. That's why you whacked him, ain't it?"

"Don't be stupid," Congo snapped. "Why would he pick the same fight he just lost?"

The cousins looked at each other. Questions filled their eyes.

"The cops took us downtown," Nicky said. "We told them all about you."

"What did they say?"

"Ask them yourself."

Phillips took a step toward the youth, but Congo put a hand on his arm. "You two understand this," he told the cousins. "We didn't kill your uncle. If the police want to discuss it with us, that's fine. But I don't want any more trouble from you."

The pair shuffled their feet, chastened. Nicky looked at the case in Phillips' hand.

"What about the rifle?"

"You won't be needing it."

"It's my old man's. He was in the Rangers. He brought it back from Panama."

"Not legally, he didn't," Congo said.

He and Phillips returned to the Cadillac. Phillips put the rifle case on the seat between them, started up and U-turned. Congo unzipped the case.

"M-16 with the serial number ground off." He removed the magazine and pulled the charging handle to extract the round from the chamber.

Phillips shot a worried glance at the weapon. "We ought to get rid of that thing."

"Sure," Congo said absently.

"I mean it, John. You shouldn't be around anything that shoots. We both know it."

Congo zipped the rifle away. "What's eating you? Last night you were bitching about never having any fun."

"This asshole situation is getting out of hand. Raymond was fine until you decided you couldn't trust anyone else to bust out his game."

"Raymond was a disaster looking for a place to happen," Congo said.

"You think the cops won't give us a shitload of grief about him?"

"I'm surprised they haven't already."

5

Two police investigators arrived without notice at Crestline's offices the next morning. The woman stood almost as tall as Congo's six feet. Her stylish jacket and close fitting designer jeans did little to soften the rangy build that would have served her well as a street officer.

"My name is Debra Long," she informed him and tucked her badge back into a shoulder bag. "My partner is Officer Yniguez."

Beyond his obvious Latin ancestry, Yniguez's features spoke of native heritage. Brown skin stretched taut over prominent cheek bones. A narrow beak and thin lips seemed a legacy of privation. A sport coat and tie worn with chinos and a checked shirt suggested he hadn't yet come to terms with the idea he had reached the white-collar world. He stood with the perfect stillness of a prehistoric hunter and measured Congo with eyes as bright and hard as obsidian.

"Would either of you like coffee?" Congo asked.

Both declined.

"No calls," Congo told Muffie and ushered them into his private office. "Sit down, please."

The two officers seated themselves side by side in chairs that faced Congo's desk. Their unhurried manner served notice the interview would last until they were satisfied.

Congo closed the door and sat behind his desk. "How can I help you?"

Debra Long put the shoulder bag on her lap. The back zipped open to make a portfolio. She consulted some paperwork.

"Before we begin, there is an identification issue. Your mother's name is recorded as Christine Morefield. Is that correct?"

Congo tensed visibly. He drew a deep breath and blew it out.

"Yes," was all he said.

"Your father is listed as not known."

"Yes."

"How did your surname come to be recorded as Congo on your birth certificate?"

"Congo is an old carnival term for a dice game. A John is a mark, a sucker."

Yniguez spoke very softly and seriously. "We are not here for your amusement, Mr. Congo. You are legally required to answer truthfully all questions about your identity."

Congo met his accusing stare directly. "All I can tell you is what I was told by people who knew my mother."

Debra Long made some entries and then turned a page. "You have an extensive record of police contact, Mr. Congo."

Silence filled the office. Sunlight slanted through the window and exposed bits of dust floating like corruption on the slow current of machine-chilled air.

"Following your discharge from military service," she said, "you went to work in a casino in Tahoe owned by a known member of organized crime."

"I was orphaned at twelve," Congo said. "The carnival where I grew up folded while I was overseas so I went to Tahoe, where some of the people had gone. They found me a job."

"Doing what?"

"Double entry bookkeeping."

She tapped her pen impatiently. "The statute of limitations has run out on anything done that long ago, Mr. Congo. You don't need to be evasive."

"I'm sorry to disappoint you, but casinos, for all their glitter and seedy reputation, are mostly statistics and accounting. I was taught my job and supervised by teetotaling Mormons."

"Is that why you left?"

"I was let go when business slowed down."

"You didn't learn much from the Mormons." She referred back to her notes. "You collected misdemeanor gambling citations in Phoenix, Denver, and San Diego."

"Youth is a time for mistakes," Congo said. "I made my share."

"After that it was cruise ships," she said. "Marked cards, shaved dice and no prosecution, because no one had jurisdiction on the high seas."

Annoyance flickered across Congo's face.

"Then Portland," she said, "where you were arrested for investigation of homicide."

"And released without being charged."

"What were you doing in Portland?"

"My business was legal."

Yniguez's eyes took on a dark glint of outrage. "Setting up another Native American casino on another reservation?"

"There was a police investigation," Congo said. "I was cleared."

"What was it you called yourself?" Yniguez asked. "Gaming consultant?"

"The man was an ex-convict," Congo said.

"Did you print business cards?" Yniguez asked. "*Have Dice Will Travel.*"

"He thought I should finger winners for him to rip off," Congo said. "I told him to forget it. He went ballistic."

A mocking smile touched Yniguez's lips. "Attention tribal leaders. No casino experience? Don't worry. Call John Congo. He'll negotiate your equipment purchases, train your staff and oversee your start-up. Everything it takes to flush a thousand years of culture down the toilet. All for a measly one percent of your first six months' gross."

Congo said nothing.

"And maybe a little skim on top of that?" Yniguez persisted. "What the hell? A bunch of dumb siwashes wouldn't know the difference. They'd probably recommend you to the next village of aborigines looking for a little extra wampum to send their scruffy papooses to school."

A vein began to throb at Congo's temple. "Did you two come here just to needle me?"

Debra Long filled in Congo's name on a field interview form. "This is a police investigation. The purpose is to ascertain the facts surrounding events at the Elysian Hotel two nights ago."

Yniguez said, "You and two of your employees broke up a dice game run by a known member of Armenian organized crime."

"I didn't know who was running the game," Congo said.

"Why did you break it up?"

"Under California Law," Congo said, "anyone who owns an interest in real property is responsible to prevent illegal activity on that property."

"Were you aware that the police were planning to raid the game that night?"

The question startled Congo. He looked from one officer to the other.

"Your little adventure cost the Department four days investigative work," Yniguez said. "Vice had a man inside. They were ready to go."

Suspicion narrowed Congo's eyes. "Why spend four days worth of the taxpayers' money on a cheap dice game your hotel squad could have taken out in forty minutes?"

Debra Long cleared her throat before her partner could retort. "Mr. Congo, we are talking about organized crime. We would appreciate your cooperation."

Congo acceded with a small shrug. "You're welcome to what little I know."

She poised her pen and nodded for him to speak.

"I went to the Elysian Hotel two nights ago to check a report of gambling and found a dice game in the executive suite. The operator told me his name was Raymond Stepanian. He offered no formal identification. I asked him to leave. He asked to be compensated. He said he was substantially indebted to loan sharks. I declined. He left the suite in the company of his two nephews, who had been assisting him with the dice game. I next saw him when he entered the hotel lobby alone and collapsed."

"You are conveniently omitting the fact that you left the scene of a homicide before the police arrived," she said.

"I didn't know a homicide had occurred. I saw only an injured man. Medical assistance was being summoned. I had no further business in the hotel, so I went home."

"Why did you make a point of mentioning loan sharks?"

"Stepanian mentioned them," Congo said. "I don't know who they might be, or if they in fact exist."

"Was Raymond Stepanian a competitor?"

"I'm no longer active in the gaming industry."

"The Elysian Hotel is your turf," she insisted. "Is the Armenian Mafia moving in?"

All pretense of courtesy vanished from Congo's voice. "If I'm a suspect in Stepanian's death, I'd like to know about it. And I'd like to call my attorney."

Debra Long took several minutes to complete her notes. She was deliberate about it, as if she hoped filling the room with oppressive silence would make Congo uncomfortable enough to blurt something further.

When it didn't, she said, "You had two employees with you in the hotel. We'll need to talk to them."

"My associates are out of the office on business. If you'll leave your number, I'll request that they contact you when they return."

She zipped her portfolio back into a shoulder bag and both investigators stood. She placed a business card on the edge of Congo's desk. Small, shiny teeth made her smile predatory.

"This has been a preliminary interview. We will be doing an in-depth follow-up once our initial review of the evidence is complete."

Congo saw the two officers out of his suite. The reassuring wink he gave Muffie was at odds with the taut muscles of his face. He closed himself back in his office and phoned Phillips and Lester in turn.

"You were a responsible property owner doing his civic duty?" Lester said sarcastically when Congo had described his own interview. "Christ, John, the cops will never buy that."

"It doesn't matter what they believe. Only what they can prove."

"John, you don't think clearly under stress. And I can feel the pressure from here."

"Just stick to the story, Les." Congo hung up.

"Muffie," he said when he came out of his office, "I'll be gone the rest of the day."

"Were they here about the man who was killed at the hotel?" Her eyes were bright and eager for details.

He stopped at the reception counter. "Look, Muffie, I know you hired on with the previous owners, and if—"

"They were just a bunch of suits."

"Well, the point is you're a great asset and I'd like you to stay, but you didn't sign up for this situation. If you're not comfortable, you're free to check out with no hard feelings. I'll write a letter of recommendation."

"I can handle it." She squared herself indignantly behind the counter.

"I hope I can," Congo said, and went out.

He rode the elevator down, brought his Porsche out of the building garage and pulled into traffic. A Buick sedan established itself a block behind him. It turned when he did.

6

The Buick followed Congo home and parked across the street. Two men sat in front, one in back. They remained in the sedan and made no attempt to conceal themselves.

Congo garaged the Porsche and changed into casual slacks and a pullover. He put an old slide action .22 Winchester rifle, eye and ear protection and two boxes of target ammunition in the Valiant. He made no effort to elude the Buick on the way to a shooting range in Little Tujunga Canyon.

One passenger left the Buick and came into the spectators' area. Muscle compacted on the man's squat frame kept a cheap suit from fitting properly. A fighter's shuffle took him to a seat behind Congo's shooting station. Congo shot with exacting care, checking each round with the range telescope.

Intense concentration combined with the visceral release of gunfire drained the tension from his body. From the range he took the Santa Ana Freeway south. The Buick stayed in his mirror through suburbs and industrial parks that spread in every direction under a brown haze.

Settlement thinned. The air grew cleaner and hotter. Low, parched hills stretched away into the distance. An off-ramp put Congo on sparsely traveled two lane blacktop where he took the speedometer needle to a hundred. The Buick had fallen back out of sight by the time he slowed for a turn. A rutted track wound its way up to a deserted cemetery.

Congo parked and found his way down among overgrown markers to the lower fence where blackberry bushes overran rotted posts and held them semierect. He went down on one knee and pulled encroaching grass away from a small granite stone that held his mother's name and dates that made her thirty two years old at her death.

"I hope you don't mind me coming to visit, Mom," he said quietly. "I know you never liked me hanging on to your skirts but the men are gone now and I thought we could have a little time together."

Congo looked up when a car door opened. The Buick had stopped behind his Valiant. The three men got out. Congo stood when one of them started down toward him.

The man was neither young nor agile. Tailored to his substantial girth was a sharkskin suit that restricted the movement of his torso. He held stubby arms out at his sides, using them like a wire walker balancing himself as he made his way down the hill in a splay-footed waddle. A silk tie was tight beneath the starched white collar of his fashionable pink shirt, so that exertion brought color to his meaty face. He arrived short of breath and spoke in a lightly accented wheeze.

"Good afternoon, Mr. Congo. My name is Gregory Demirjian. Raymond Stepanian was my nephew."

Demirjian had full lips and limpid eyes and shiny hair that once had been black. His presence was aromatic, as if the dampness on his jowls was cologne rather than a film of sweat. The hand he offered was moist. Congo shook it only briefly.

"I didn't shoot your nephew, if that's why you're following me around."

A miniature smile curved Demirjian's lips. "Call it a small test of your moral fiber. To see whether you would run or fight or simply go on about your business."

"You must have a lot of time on your hands."

"You will pardon my curiosity, but I need to understand. You went just now to a shooting range. It confuses me that a businessman would interrupt his day for such a trifle."

"I needed to blow off steam," Congo said.

"On the way here you drove dangerously fast, but—"

"I didn't shoot Raymond."

"Please," Demirjian said, "that is not why I came."

"Why, then?"

Demirjian drew himself up to his full five feet eight inches. "I loaned my nephew twenty thousand dollars to capitalize the little enterprise you broke up. It is now up to you to make good my loss."

Congo snapped his fingers. "All in the family," he said with a sly wink. "Blood is the best security."

"Do you think this is a joke, Mr. Congo?"

"Let me tell you what I think happened, and you can correct me if I'm wrong."

Demirjian lapsed into cagey silence.

"Raymond came to you for money," Congo said. "He told you he had a concession to operate a dice game in the Elysian Hotel. He needed cash to buy a layout and bank the game. Based on my two minute talk with Raymond, he would have been skinned alive if he went out to buy gaming equipment on the open market. But as a lender you have reciprocal collection agreements with people in Nevada. You called your contacts, got a deal on a used layout and a gross of shaved dice and paid the supplier directly so Raymond wouldn't be tempted into any folly."

Demirjian sighed heavily. "Raymond was always the handsome, charming boy. I'm afraid we coddled him when he was younger."

"So naturally you sent him to the hotel with only one night's bank. When the game was over, he brought the receipts straight to you. You gave him a fresh stake the next night. He had to earn out his weekly interest before he saw any return from the game."

Cunning lit Demirjian's eyes. "You seem exceptionally well informed."

"Raymond's nephews didn't snitch you off," Congo assured him. "I used to operate dice games."

"Then you understand the importance of repaying the twenty thousand dollars I loaned my nephew."

"I'll look at repaying what you actually lent," Congo offered, "as soon as I have the invoice for the gaming equipment, a copy of your ledgers for the three full nights the game operated and the name of whoever granted the concession to operate in the Elysian Hotel."

Demirjian dismissed the idea with a wheezy chuckle. "You cannot expect me to believe this"—he waved a pudgy hand—"this proposal of yours?"

"If I pay for the equipment, I'm entitled to the invoice."

"An invoices which establish the interstate transport of gaming equipment. A Federal offense, Mr. Congo, as you must know."

"I know you wouldn't have been foolish enough to use your own name."

"And my ledgers. Those are evidence of usury under a legal system put in place by banks that do not appreciate competition from entrepreneurs like myself."

"Do you want to deal or don't you?"

The corners of Demirjian's mouth drew down in disapproval. "Sir, you are fortunate that I do not ask for more than the return of my capital. Your activities may well have been the proximate cause of my nephew's death."

"Proximate cause, my ass. If Raymond had driven a bus or sold appliances, he'd still be alive."

"I have had considerable trouble over this little business."

"For which you charged your nephew twenty percent interest a week," Congo said. "I don't imagine you have a family rate."

Demirjian's eyes were eloquent with injury. "I made an honest effort to teach Raymond the rules of the world he would have to face when I was no longer here to assist him. You are trying to take advantage of my charity."

"If you want me to cover your losses, I want the supporting bookkeeping and the name of anyone against whom I have recourse."

"And what is to stop you from having the police in attendance when I present my documentation?"

Congo tensed at the word 'police'. He looked down at Demirjian's shoes; midnight blue suede against the withered brown grass.

"The grave you're standing on belongs to my mother."

Demirjian took a startled step backward. "I am truly sorry. I did not know."

"She was killed not far from here."

"Believe me, Mr. Congo, I had no wish to desecrate your—"

"She was a carnival stripper," Congo recalled and his eyes lost focus. "Trouble with local men was nothing unusual but one night it got out of hand. A roustabout heard her screaming and caught her attacker. He turned out to be the son of the local police chief. It wasn't the boy's first trouble. He was one wrong step away from prison."

Tremors rippled through the small muscles of Congo's face and his words were no longer conversation but pent up emotions venting themselves.

"The boy's father brought an iron bar into our trailer and chased out me and the two women who were helping my mother. I could hear him hitting her. I could see the trailer shudder from the fury of it. I tried to go to her, but a cop had me by the arm. When I kicked him to try to get away, he hit me harder than I had ever been hit before."

Congo stopped trembling and focused on Demirjian, as if he had just that second realized he was there. Emotion faded into recollection.

"I was lying on my back. The grass was wet. I was too stunned to move. I could see the Ferris wheel turn. Music was playing and people were laughing. The carnival was running full blast while my mother was being beaten to death. It didn't seem real. Like some of bizarre nightmare. Like everything would be all right if I could just break the spell. Just wake up. Just—"

Congo unhooked his spectacles and massaged the bridge of his nose. When he replaced the glasses his face was serene, his veneer intact.

"I never saw my mother again. The coffin was sealed when they buried her. The roustabout who tried to help her went to prison for her murder."

Demirjian allowed a brief silence to be sure Congo had stabilized, then spoke with quiet sympathy. "You are an intelligent man. You would not judge all police on the basis of one misguided official desperate to protect his own wayward child."

"I was twelve years old," Congo said. "The hatred and fear were seared in. I wouldn't go to the police. I have enough trouble tolerating them when they come to me."

Demirjian eyed him shrewdly. "Earlier you said you were blowing off steam. Did your stress have anything to do with police contact?"

"I was interviewed this morning."

"In regard to Raymond?"

"They were upset with me for breaking up his game. They were planning to raid it that night."

"This is true? You are not lying?" Demirjian's eyes fixed on Congo's, compelling candor. "It is most important that I know."

"They had known about the game for four days."

Worried thoughts surfaced in Demirjian's eyes. He drew inward, fell silent.

"Do you want to tell me about it?" Congo asked.

"It is a small matter. I shall attend to it."

"There is nothing small about any of this, Mr. Demirjian. Your nephew is dead. My investment in the Elysian Hotel may be in peril."

"I leave you now with your mother. I offer apologies for my intrusion. I hope your visit is a comfort to you."

"How can I get in touch with you?"

"I shall contact you. I would not like to hear that you are looking for me. I am sorry to sound melodramatic but my business does require precautions."

Demirjian made his splay-footed way back up the hill. The quiet wheeze of his exertion was the only sound in the hot, still afternoon. He got into the rear of the Buick. His men got in front and they drove away. Cologne lingered on the breathless air, a cloying memory of his visit. Congo looked down at the head stone, then away at a distant rise where a tiny road grader worked, toy-like in its quiet.

"I'll have to move you pretty soon, Mom," he said softly and contritely. "I know this is your place, out here on the old carnival circuit, and I hate to take you away, but they're coming now, the people who build things and own things, and I don't think they'll let you stay. I'm one of them now, like I always wanted to be, but I remember your favorite things and I'll do the best I can for you."

He hiked back up to the Valiant and returned to the bustle of L.A. It was mid-afternoon when he stopped at the Elysian Hotel for a late lunch at a window table in the coffee shop. He ate at a leisurely pace until flashing blue strobes caught his eye. A police cruiser rolled up to the hotel's main door. Congo signaled for his check and went out to where a small crowd had gathered.

A television news camera videotaped uniformed police officers escorting two handcuffed women from an elevator out the main door. Young and attractive, both wore chic business attire that would allow them to pass with little notice anywhere downtown.

A boy in the crowd tugged at a woman's arm. "Hey, Mom, how come those babes are getting busted?"

Amused eyes turned and the woman flushed. "Matthew, what have I told you about that kind of language?"

"But how come they're getting busted?"

"We have to meet your father." She hustled him off.

The police cruiser pulled away. The crowd dissipated.

Congo went to the telephone bank and pressed out a number.

"My name is John Congo. I'd like to speak to Royce Hillman."

"I'm sorry, sir. Mr. Hillman is not in."

"All right, Pat Easter then." He watched the TV camera set up for an interview while he waited.

"Pat Easter, John," came the enthusiastic voice. "How can I help you?"

"The police just hauled two hookers out of the Elysian Hotel in time for the videotape to lead off the five o-clock news. I want to know what's going on."

Easter made his voice sympathetic. "John, you sound distressed."

"I already know how I feel."

"Perhaps we should talk."

"Fine. I can be there in twenty minutes."

"Well, I'm afraid my first opening isn't until eight tomorrow morning. If that's too early, we could—"

"I'll see you at eight." Congo hung up.

7

Congo tapped a tightly rolled newspaper against his trouser leg and stared down from the window of Hillman Management's 42nd floor reception area. Miniature vehicles jammed the Harbor Freeway, locked in a brutal morning commute. Smog hung like poison gas over no-man's land. Congo glanced at the receptionist.

"Would you remind Mr. Easter that his eight o'clock appointment is here?"

"Sir, I've already—"

"John! Good morning!" Pat Easter strode into the reception area, offering an enthusiastic smile and an outstretched hand. "How are you?"

"Running short of patience."

"I am sorry. Something came up at the last minute."

"Like persuading Eyewitness News to take the Elysian Hotel prostitution arrests out of lead position in their next broadcast?"

"John, can we discuss this in my office?"

Easter held court in a spacious corner dominated by a baronial desk. He seated Congo in a facing chair and made himself comfortable in a high-backed leather swivel.

"Now, John, how can I help you?"

Congo unrolled his newspaper and read from an article. "… following a series of surprise raids, Prosecutors charged former actress and model Catherine 'China Doll' Carson with operating a prostitution ring. Court documents allege that escorts would meet executives and entertainment industry figures at the city's most prominent lodging, including the prestigious Elysian Hotel"—he looked significantly at Easter—"where two were arrested yesterday."

Easter spread his hands in a helpless gesture. "The average guest count at the Elysian is greater than the population of many California towns. A few unfortunate incidents are unavoidable."

"Why did the police make the arrests at the Elysian?"

"The women happened to be there, I suppose."

"Why parade them out through the lobby?"

Easter shrugged.

"And how did the news media know when to set up their cameras?"

"John, don't you think you're blowing one small incident out of proportion?"

"Isn't that what Clinton's lawyers said, just before Congress impeached him?" Easter managed a pained laugh.

Congo's features turned to stone. "Look, Pat," he said in a voice taut with stifled anger, "I'm going to tell you right here and now"—he glanced around his posh surroundings—"closed up in your fancy office where nobody can hear us and it won't tarnish the executive polish in front of the toadies, that I don't find one damned thing about this situation the least bit funny."

Easter's smile was an emphatic display of tolerance. "It's just that I think you're having trouble seeing the big picture."

"I was raised in a gypsy carnival, where people had to hustle for every nickel."

"You're a property owner now, John." Easter tilted his chair back toward a wall of polished plaques attesting to his years of success and his energetic service in various worthy causes. "In fact you are in a position where you could be a positive force for change in Los Angeles."

"What is this? Con job 101? Empower the mark? Make him feel important if he does what you want?"

Easter blinked.

"You know, Pat, I'm feeling a little insulted here. First you let me stew in reception to soften me up. Then you let me blow off steam. Now you're getting ready to hit me with the pitch. I mean, Jesus Christ, they taught me this stuff in the carnival when I was eight years old."

"I'm not sure what you want me to say, John."

"Let's start with the truth about the dice game."

"Is this an obsession with you, John?"

"The dice game was the opening move in a police sting operation, wasn't it? The target was a man named Gregory Demirjian."

Silence committed Easter to nothing.

"Demirjian is a loan shark," Congo went on. "A player in the Armenian Mafia. His Achilles' heel was a half-smart nephew named Raymond Stepanian. Raymond had a loopy idea about putting a dice game into the Elysian Hotel with Uncle Gregory's financial backing. The police approached Hillman Management for cooperation in trapping Demirjian. You let the game into the hotel and wound up with Raymond dead in the lobby."

Easter's tone was sage. "We've found that the long term benefits of cooperating with the police far outweigh any short term inconvenience."

Congo frowned skeptically. "Maybe I'd better take this situation up with the other owners."

Easter rippled nervous fingers on the arm of his chair. "We're, uh, not anxious for this to get out."

"That comes as no surprise."

Congo rolled his newspaper. Easter raised a hand before he could stand.

"If you'll allow us to share some confidential information with you, I think you'll understand why."

Congo looked dubious but acquiesced with a small gesture. Easter escorted him to a conference room. The room was windowless and elegant, filled with a hush that could only mean a heavy sound blanket behind the paneled walls. Things said there were meant to stay there. Easter left Congo briefly alone and returned smiling.

"Royce will join us in a minute," he said, and his voice fell to a tantalizing register. "He's talking to one of his classmates from Yale. Royce's class has come to prominence in business, finance, government. All the places where it helps to have a receptive ear."

Hillman opened the door and strode in just on cue. His moon face lit up and he thrust out a hand.

"John, good to see you again."

Congo stood with an impatient, "Sure," and shook hands with the executive.

Hillman held his grip, using a hand at Congo's elbow to steer him to the end of a mahogany table where he installed him in a comfortable chair.

"John, so far you've focused on the problems a hotel can encounter. Have you thought about its possibilities as an agent of growth?"

Easter slid back a panel to reveal a large white board. The room lights dimmed and a low pitched hum emanated from a three-lens projector hung beneath the ceiling. A logo appeared on the white board, the name *Athens* in formal capitals backed by the fluted limestone columns of a classical Greek temple.

"The twin principles of strength in numbers and economy of scale are as old as civilization," Easter said as computer animation drew back an imaginary camera to reveal an ancient city at the height of its glory. "The original city-states arose because men discovered they could accomplish more with less by combining their assets and talents. The same principles apply to modern real estate."

Ancient Athens dissolved into contemporary Los Angeles. An imaginary camera zoomed in on a cluster of downtown high-rise buildings.

"If a group of property owners pool their holdings, judicious re-financing can yield enough cash to add other comparable properties to the pooled portfolio and turn idle equity into growth assets."

"Judicious re-financing," Congo repeated, drawing out the words as if he were tasting something unpleasant. "Can you be a little more specific?"

"It's no different from re-financing your home," Easter assured him. "You take out a larger mortgage at a better rate, pay off the old loan and have cash left over to do what you want."

"What are you planning to do with the cash from re-financing the Elysian?" Congo asked.

"Not just from the Elysian," Hillman announced in a voice that resonated with pride of authorship. "Hillman Management will be re-capitalized under the name Athens. Athens will issue shares of common stock representing the total value of Hillman and the ten major properties currently managed by Hillman. Those shares will be exchanged for the ownership interests in the properties. Once all ten properties are under the Athens umbrella, they can be re-financed as a group. That will generate enough excess cash to purchase at least two and probably three additional major properties."

Congo looked in disbelief from one executive to the other. "Let me get this straight. You're suggesting that I hand over stock in the Elysian Hotel worth more than two million dollars in return for shares in this Athens—a company I've never heard of until this morning—so you can go on a shopping trip?"

"As a shareholder in Athens," Hillman said, "you will still own an interest in the Elysian Hotel. And nine other major properties. A portfolio worth well over one billion dollars. Plus"—his small eyes glittered—"an interest in the new properties bought with the proceeds of re-financing."

"A bigger mortgage," Congo observed, "means bigger mortgage payments and less money left over to pay dividends."

"Dividend policy will be set by the Athens board," Hillman said.

Questions rose in Congo's eyes and morphed into a frown. "Is there some paperwork that goes with all this? A proposal or prospectus or something? The last time my credit card company changed their agreement, I got three pages of fine print."

Hillman made a vague, apologetic gesture. "To comply with the law, and to be fair, we will be sending the proposal to all the owners at the same time by registered mail. We're meeting with you this morning as a courtesy, to clear up your concerns."

Easter turned off the projector. "John, I don't understand your reluctance. This deal is being put together for the benefit of the owners. If I were in your shoes, I'd be elated."

"Try surprised," Congo suggested. "I've just been told I'm part of a billion dollar transaction. A deal I've heard nothing about until now, in spite of the fact you've obviously been hatching it for some time."

Easter coughed uncomfortably. "We wanted to bring the owners along in the planning process, of course, but it just wasn't possible."

Hillman nodded gravely. "Had our competitors gotten wind of this, they would have done everything possible to frustrate it."

Both executives eyed Congo, clearly trying to gauge how much of a threat he posed to their secrets. His hostility dissolved into a bland, accommodating smile.

"Well, I'm not saying I won't sign on. Particularly if the money looks right."

Hillman's meaty face shone with delight. "That's the spirit."

Easter chimed in with, "We can count on your support, then?"

"I'll be looking forward to reading your proposal."

Hillman gave a satisfied nod. "And remember, John, this morning's discussion is in strict confidence."

"Of course."

There were smiles and handshakes all around. Easter escorted Congo out to the reception area. Rachel Lee Krebs was behind the counter, collecting invoices from the morning mail. She saw Congo and hurried away.

Congo drove directly to his own office suite and put his newspaper on the reception counter. "Muffie, there's a lawyer's name in the article on the escort service arrests. Call him, please. Give him my name. Tell him I need to talk to Catherine Carson alone, as soon as he can arrange it."

Muffie's eyes lit up. This wasn't just business. She was on the team. She seized the paper and devoured the article.

8

Time had begun to crack the alabaster beauty that was China Doll Carson's trademark. She dressed as if style could make up the difference; high boots and jodhpurs, a robins egg blue turtleneck and a suede sport jacket buttoned against the blustery wind that brought the smell of salt water and kelp off the Pacific.

"I hope you don't mind sand in your wingtips," she said.

Congo managed a smile through the chill. "What man hasn't dreamed of walking the beach at Malibu with a show business goddess?"

By law California shore lands were public, even near the enclaves of the elite. This morning low clouds dark with impending rain overhung miles of pristine sand, chasing away all but the two of them.

"They booked me into the L.A. County jail," she said, and shivered at the memory. "When I got out, all I could think of was breathing clean air."

"Do you want to tell me about it?"

"Jail?"

"The Elysian Hotel."

A tiny smile touched her lips. "It's ironic that it ended because of a hotel. Maybe all of us wind up back where we started."

Congo's look of polite curiosity didn't conceal his impatience.

"I was just out of high school," she explained, "working a shift at a concierge desk. Sometimes I got to help celebrities. People I'd seen only in magazines. In the articles they were just what you said. Goddesses. But up close they were nothing special. No better than me. Big hair and a Tijuana boob job and I could make it too. And if I didn't, what the hell? I'd go to beauty school or learn bookkeeping or something. I wouldn't be any worse off than if I never tried."

A bit of paper trash scooted past along the sand, blown this way and that, borne on the gusts of chance. She watched it soar a couple of hopeful feet then fall back to be battered along like tumbleweed. Sadness muted her voice.

"Now the implants are gone, the hair is back to wash and wear and I'm on my way to prison."

"Why me?" Congo asked. "You and I talked once. Maybe twenty minutes in all. Years ago."

"I was a washed-up actress," she recalled, "shooting the last episode of a can-celled series. You were a pissed off casino boss. You taught me to deal just so you could hurry production along and get the film crew off your gaming floor."

"Don't sell yourself short," he said. "I remember being a little star struck."

"You were so damn insistent I do it right. I asked if gambling was your work or your religion. You said you were just doing it to raise a stake. You wanted to settle down, buy your own piece of the world."

"You didn't carry my dream around all that time."

"I forgot you as soon as we left the location," she confessed. "Then one night I was playing solitaire and I caught myself dealing the way you taught me. Shuffle the cards flat to the table. Deliver low to the surface. Develop a rhythm so the other players can't read anything into your movements. It all came back to me."

Congo stopped and stared out at the white-capped ocean. "Was Royce Hill-man a client of your service?"

"Until he wanted me to blackmail my other clients."

Wind flattened their clothing against them. She moved close to him for warmth.

"Royce had a plan. He needed leverage. To persuade the right people to—"

"When you called and told me about the Crestline bankruptcy," Congo said, adrift in his own thoughts, "about a share in the Elysian Hotel being available, I went to an attorney. A specialist in those things. He told me not to bother. The Elysian was a major property. The judge would never let any ownership interest fall into questionable hands. My offer would be disqualified on grounds of moral turpitude."

"I knew it wouldn't be easy," she said. "I needed someone driven by a dream and a single-minded passion. Someone who wouldn't give up, no matter what. I guess that's what I remembered most about you. Why I remembered you out of all the thousands of men I've met."

"When we heard the offer had been accepted," Congo said, "the attorney turned white. Never offered another word of advice. Just completed the paper-work and got out of my life."

"I'd like to walk some more," she said.

"The attorney knew the judge had been fixed," Congo said as they set off. "He thought I'd done it. That's what scared him. But the judge was your client. You used your hold over him to make sure my offer wouldn't be rejected out of hand. Hillman wanted you to back his proposal. You recruited me instead."

Anger etched confirmation into the tiny muscles of her face. "Royce was all smiles and promises. He had this empire he was going to build. He needed one big property, a 'crown jewel' he called it, to start the ball rolling. The Elysian Hotel was his choice. It had the most fragmented ownership and the Crestline shares were in bankruptcy. He wanted me to use my influence, as he put it, with the bankruptcy judge and then help him persuade the other owners to go along with his plan."

"What is his plan?" Congo asked. "I mean, did he give you any details?"

"I didn't want any. I knew who would get the blame if anything went wrong. I thought if you took over Crestline his scheme would fall apart. He'd go away and leave me alone. You and I would both get what we wanted."

Congo's, "Yeah," was cool and sardonic.

He watched a gull circle and swoop in the distance. The bird was trying to get at something on the ground, first spreading broad wings to play the wind gusts and then flapping and diving to fight them, never quite figuring out how to reach the prize.

"I understand why you couldn't expose Hillman when he came to you," Congo said. "Disclosing any client name would send every other client running. You'd be all escorts and no service. But what's stopping you now?"

"The court has sealed my client list to prevent what they politely call 'irreparable harm' to people who haven't been convicted of anything."

"Hillman pressured the police to bust you," Congo realized, "to make sure you could never expose him."

She kicked apart a clump of damp sand. "The police can bust blue collar johns and post them on the Internet. I go straight back to jail if I rat out the social register for the same thing."

"What can you tell me about Hillman?" Congo asked.

She put her head down and hunched her shoulders, drifting a couple of feet away as they walked. "Another Hollywood madam bites the dust. No big deal. The names change but the pussy stays the same."

"Come on, Catherine. Feeling sorry for yourself won't help you or me. Hillman has powerful contacts, he's a couple ants short of a picnic and we're both in his way. Give me something I can use against him."

She gave Congo a withering look. "If I had anything, I'd use it myself. I hate what he's done to me. All my life I've been able to scratch and claw. Now I'm in a damn fish bowl. I have to mind my manners while lawyers do their best to pick me clean. My only hope is to convert my assets into cash and jewelry and stash them until I've done my time and cut my deal with the IRS."

"Can you talk to the escorts Hillman saw?" Congo asked. "Find out what he said to them? Keep your ears open for any common theme?"

She dismissed his naiveté with a hopeless shake of her head. "Escorts make their money by listening, not hearing. They're picking up voice inflection cues. Looking for when to shut up and smile and when to stroke the ego. The actual conversation is in one ear and out the other."

It was Congo's turn to sulk.

"So we're back where we started," she said. "I'm washed up and you're pissed off."

"I'm not pissed off."

A sudden lull in the wind amplified the irritability in his voice. The rush of cars passing unseen up on Highway 1 became audible. Waves crashed ashore in a gurgle of foam then receded, like innocence ebbing away.

"You know," Congo said, "I came to L.A. to clean up my life. To prove that I was better than my past. That I could do it right if I just had the chance. Christ, I was better off when I was hustling. At least I wasn't mixed up in any federal crimes."

The wind picked up and she moved closer again. "I needed help," she said. "I didn't know where else to turn."

"Nothing personal," Congo said. "Just blind chance. Chaos theory."

"Excuse me?"

"Chaos theory is the law of unknowable interactions and unpredictable consequences. It's mathematically possible for a butterfly to flap its wings in China and set off a chain reaction that blows a hurricane into the Caribbean. But the chain is so complex it can't be discerned from chaos and the probability is so low it would never be predicted. Like the two of us talking for a few minutes years ago and winding up here."

"Where did you get that?" she asked. "Public television?"

"I spent my life in the gaming industry. It was my business to learn the mechanics of chance."

"What will you do now?" she asked.

"What I started out to do. Clean up my act. It just dawned on me that means changing the habits of a lifetime."

"No, I mean what are you going to do about Royce?"

All Congo had to offer was an apologetic shrug. "You're on your own there. I'll have my hands full trying to stabilize Crestline."

She hunched her shoulders and her voice retreated into disappointment. "My lawyer told me not to talk to you."

"He was right," Congo said. "If anyone connects the dots in the Crestline bankruptcy, we're both toast."

Her smile could not have been tinier. "Does that mean I take the rest of my walk alone?"

"There are no hard feelings," he said. "I got what I asked for. It's up to me to make the most of it."

They wished each other luck and parted company.

9

Muted laughter greeted Congo when the elevator door opened on his floor. He followed it to his office suite and found his three employees gathered in the reception area.

Phillips nudged Abe Lester. "Dat's da Big Boy, awright," he said out of the side of his mouth.

"Dis muz be de plaize, den," Lester said huskily.

Both men guffawed.

Muffie sat tittering behind the reception counter.

Congo gave her a look. "Hash brownies?"

She sobered instantly and shook her head. "I only did that the once. When the owners before went bankrupt and I thought I was out of work."

Phillips nudged Lester again. "Think he'll make us take the blood oath?"

"I'm okay with getting my finger pricked, but I don't know about holding the burning paper in my hand."

"If I ever betrays dis ting of ours," Phillips intoned, "I will boin like dis paper boins."

The two men laughed hard enough to bring tears.

Congo eyed them dubiously. "When you two get through slow dancing, why don't you come in the office and tell me about it."

They followed him in and all three sat down.

"We just got back from the cops," Phillips said.

"I'm glad somebody enjoyed them," Congo said.

Lester shook his head in disbelief. "You should have heard them."

Phillips choked down a spasm of laughter. "They asked if you had Raymond hit."

"Hit?"

Phillips made a boy scout salute. "Honest to God. That's the word they used."

Lester nodded. "I think they found your name in the Nevada Black Book."

"They think you're the biggest gambler on the coast," Phillips said.

"They don't know you're just a lovable grift artist and chiseler who saved his pennies," Lester said.

Congo made a face.

"Who's Murray the Camel, anyway?" Phillips asked.

"Was," Congo corrected. "He's long dead."

"Okay, so who was he?"

"A player in the Chicago underworld," Congo said. "He was some kind of silent owner in the first place I worked in Tahoe."

Phillips and Lester exchanged glances.

"Our lovable chiseler really was mobbed up."

"Did Murray the Camel have one hump or two?"

"For Christ's sake," Congo said, "I never met the man. What else what did the police ask you?"

"That was pretty much it," Lester said.

"They think you came here to muscle in on the local rackets," Phillips said.

Frustration compressed Congo's mouth. "All right. Thanks, guys."

The two men stood to leave.

Lester said, "I'm going to get one of those license plate frames that say *Mafia Staff Car.*"

Phillips started to laugh then remembered something. "Oh, hey, John, how does it look for a couple of days off?"

Congo was rolling the drawings he had prepared for Karen Steele. "Does it have to be now?"

"Eileen gets in tomorrow. It's a two day sales trip."

Congo secured the roll with rubber bands. "I thought she re-married."

"We're just getting together for dinner and a movie."

"Do me a favor. Limit the vacation to just the time you're together."

Lester's eyes narrowed. "What aren't you telling us, John?"

Congo set the plans aside and stood, straightening his suit coat. "Royce Hillman wants to take over the properties his company manages. Including the Elysian."

Phillips snorted. "Tell him to fuck off."

"According to my lawyer," Congo said, "if Hillman can get fifty one percent of the shares to go along, it's a done deal unless I can prove fraud or undue influence."

"So what do we do?" Lester asked.

"Go back to teaching our Native American brothers the white man's way?" Phillips rolled a pair of imaginary dice.

"About the Elysian, nothing until Hillman makes his move. But we better fill the Crestline vacancies fast. Just in case we lose the hotel dividends."

Congo shooed them out of his office. He checked his reflection in the glass covering the worn carnival poster on the wall and tucked the roll of plans under his arm.

◆　　◆　　◆

Crestline Shopping Plaza formed a horseshoe around an asphalt parking area. Noon hour sun raised steam from puddles of morning rain. Congo picked up a discarded soft drink cup and dropped it in a trash receptacle on his way to the Mexican restaurant. A chattering hostess escorted him back to one of the small tables crowded into faux stucco niches. Karen Steele arrived a few minutes after twelve. Even constrained by decorum and three inch heels, she made excellent time back to his table.

"I am sorry, traffic was just a nightmare," she said in a breathless rush, seating herself before he could stand to draw back a chair, filling the space around her with vibrant energy and a subtle hint of jasmine, moving condiments so he could unroll the center plan. She danced a polished fingernail on a back corner marked *vacant*.

"This is your major challenge. Big space with very little frontage. To a retailer, exposure is money."

"It's been a tough sell," he agreed.

"The other is food service."

Congo glanced around. "This place may not have much in the way of upscale ambiance, but the enchiladas are pretty good. Of course, if you'd rather eat somewhere else—?"

A laugh bubbled up from her throat. "What I mean is, you have five food service vendors in the center."

"Too many?"

"For a center this size, the maximum is probably three. You'd better plan on losing at least two within the year."

Congo nodded reluctant agreement. "I can tell you from the accounts receivable aging report which two."

"We'd better tour them along with the vacant space."

Karen rolled the drawings and secured them between the handles of a leather case that stood upright on the floor beside her. A waitress arrived and she ordered the Guadalajara Caesar.

"Between working out at lunch and grabbing fast food with the boys on the way back from activities, I never get enough nutrition."

"I admire your energy," Congo said after he had ordered a chicken enchilada and a glass of milk. "Raising two boys alone can't be easy."

Flattery brought a brief flush and a modest shake of her head. "Their dad lives in Orange County. He's taking them to the Angels' game tonight. At ten and twelve, a strong role model is really important."

"My experience is on the other end of the single parent situation," Congo confessed.

Curiosity filled her eyes. "It must have been exciting traveling with a carnival when you were young."

"Mostly it was lonely," he recalled. "I was trapped in a parallel universe behind the glare and the tinny music. Carnival people don't belong in the towns they play. Even toddling into a store with my mother when I was little, I could feel it. When I was older, it meant no school and no kids my age."

"No school?" She eyed him skeptically.

"Only when the truant officer was diligent. Otherwise my mother taught me."

"She must have been well educated, if she was able to home school you."

"When you're a kid, you don't think to ask about the past," Congo said. "When I asked if we would ever have a place of our own, she told me the carnival was our place and I should be glad I was free from the hypocrisy that went with the straight world."

"Hypocrisy?" Karen asked. "The straight world?"

"That mindset is critical to a scam artist," Congo explained. "It allows him to shift blame to the mark and feel positive about what he's doing. Card mechanics practice bottom dealing in front of a mirror until it becomes so natural they can't see themselves cheat."

"Well, you've got me totally paranoid about carnivals," she said with a nervous laugh. "I'll never ride another Ferris wheel."

"It's not about carnivals. The principles are the same whether you're peddling five shots for a quarter on a toy animal no one can win or manipulating corporate stock. The stuffed shirts in the corner offices can't see themselves cheating any more than the card sharp watching the mirror. They think they're adding value for the investors."

Karen tucked a stray tendril of hair behind one ear and smiled tentatively, as if she weren't sure where the conversation was going.

"Sorry," Congo blurted. "I'm being a bore. You came to talk business."

They spent lunch discussing the center's financial structure. The noon crowd was beginning to dissipate when they left the restaurant. Walking past storefronts, Karen kept up a running commentary about displays that looked too busy or used color badly or committed one of the other retailing blunders she was attuned to. She spoke at overwhelming speed. Congo wrote quickly and got only part of it.

They came to an empty window filled by a poster advertising the space for lease. Congo unlocked a door and fumbled on the lights.

A cavern resolved itself out of the dimness, still crowded with shelving left by the last tenant. A fluorescent tube sizzled ominously in a ceiling fixture. Several others had burned out.

"Those need to be replaced," Karen said.

She toured with an expert eye, careful of her pumps and hosiery in the mine-field of carpet rips and fallen pieces of metal trim.

"You'll probably want to strip away the old furnishings," she suggested. "Empty space looks bigger."

"I thought someone might want to save some re-fit money," Congo offered.

"A store is a big part of the owners' lives," she said. "They want to put their signature on it."

"I begin to see why I haven't set the commercial real estate world on fire."

Congo took out his cell phone, allowing Karen to drift away while he pressed the speed dial code for Clint Phillips.

"What's up, John?"

"You know my bright idea about leaving the shelving in the southwest corner space at the center?"

"Not everyone is as cheap as you, John."

"The word is thrifty. Can you find a contractor to clean this stuff out pronto?"

"What's the rush?"

"We may have a chance to lease the—"

A scream cut him off. Karen stood at the rear of the space, staring out an open door.

"Later, Phil." Congo cut the connection and covered the distance in a dozen strides. "What is it?"

Her mouth worked without producing a sound.

Congo looked out into an alley that served as the center's delivery and trash removal access. A wiry old man in filthy clothing was climbing out of a nearby dumpster, clutching a large piece of cardboard. He scrambled down from the dumpster and retreated to a shopping cart crammed with plastic trash bags full of who-knew-what. Keeping a wary eye on Congo and Karen, he stowed his ill-got-ten treasure. Doddering movements held down speed but he wheeled the clumsy cart away with all the concentration of an escaping bank robber.

"God!" Karen breathed, and took Congo's arm. "My heart is still pounding. I opened the door and the first thing I saw was the lid come up and a head pop out. What a start."

Congo smiled at her closeness. "Dumpster diving is pretty hard to stop, but I'll talk to the security contractor."

She released him, embarrassed at her impulse. "Well, that should do it for this space, anyway."

He secured the rear door. "I'll try to get it cleared out this afternoon."

"I'll need a key to show it."

"If you're free for dinner tonight, I can have an extra made by then."

Her smile was apologetic.

"The boys are going to the baseball game," he persisted. "You'll be eating alone … unless you're seeing someone."

"Perhaps I'd better let you know."

It was far enough from refusal to allow him to accede with a gracious nod. He secured the door and they set off to tour the problem food service vendors.

10

Congo blended with the evening shadows almost to the point that he could fade into them and vanish. He passed silently into the *Blue Heron* restaurant.

A little money got his table assignment changed to a secluded window location. He declined service and stared away down the coast, visible as a meandering line of separation between the sea of lights beginning to fill the Los Angeles basin and the final shimmer of sunset on the Pacific.

Karen Steele arrived a fashionable fifteen minutes late. She had selected a magenta cocktail sheath that suggested more than it revealed. Congo wasn't the only man who watched her cross the dining floor. He stood smiling while the maitre'd drew back a chair and seated her.

"I'm glad you called," Congo said. "I was afraid my invitation was too abrupt."

She put him at ease with a musical laugh. "That was just me being defensive. Pure knee jerk. As soon as I remembered the leftover pizza in the fridge, I came to my senses."

A server arrived with dinner rolls and condescended to review the specials. The swordfish intrigued Karen. Her eyes chided Congo for his lack of adventure when he ordered a shrimp Creole buried in the menu. She declined wine in favor of an exotic tea. As soon as the server was gone, her voice fell to a confidential register.

"I understand you met with Royce Hillman and Pat Easter."

Surprise narrowed Congo's eyes. "Have I been sworn to secrecy over something everyone else already knows?"

Her laugh was only a little nervous. "The real estate industry runs on gossip. Secrets just don't keep well." She favored him with an envious smile. "Particularly something as exciting as the Athens concept."

His only response was a noncommittal shrug.

"With no effort at all," she said, "you'll go from owning just a share in the Elysian Hotel to an equity interest in a major portfolio."

Congo's gaze drifted to the night lit city. "I remember the first time I saw L.A. I was four, maybe five. My mother and I rode up with the man who owned the carnival. He was a bottom feeder in organized crime. Looking back, I suppose he needed a ready-made family for some scam. All I knew at the time was he drove the shiniest car I ever saw. A three tone DeSoto with skyscraper tail fins. I remember kneeling on the back seat with my nose against the window watching the parade of buildings as we rolled up the Santa Ana Freeway. We ate lunch in a real restaurant. I had a peanut butter sandwich and potato chips and a glass of milk so big I could barely get my hands around it. When we got back that night, I was so excited I couldn't sleep."

His rambling was far enough from the topic of conversation to leave Karen staring.

"Owning a piece of L.A. is personal with me," he explained. "I don't want to be just a name on a list of shareholders."

"It's not enough, you know."

"What isn't?"

"Buying Crestline. Settling down."

"It's enough for me."

"L.A. isn't just the buildings you saw when you were little. It's people. A community. Built on trust and a willingness to work for the future. If you think like a carnival sharper you'll always be a carnival sharper, no matter what you own or where you settle."

"Not all the sharpers are in carnivals," he said.

"What does that mean?"

"Hillman put a dice game into the Elysian to panic the owners into going along with the Athens deal."

"Where did you hear that?"

"I found the game. If I hadn't thrown it out, a police raid would have spread the hotel all over the news media."

"Thrown it out?" She appraised his trim build with eyes that doubted him prone to anything seriously physical.

"Figure of speech," he said. "The players were cooperative. They left when we asked." He grinned to assure her the whole episode had been cordial.

She began picking apart a dinner roll, a suggestion that she was taking the situation apart in her mind. "How would a dice game panic the owners into accepting the Athens proposal?"

"Remember the little man who popped out of the dumpster?"

She offered an uneasy smile. "I hope you didn't get the wrong impression. I really don't frighten that easily."

"Sure you do. So do I. You saw the little man and freaked. I heard you scream and jumped out of my skin. It's a natural reaction. Our species never would have survived the saber-toothed tigers without it."

"It was just the surprise of seeing him," she insisted.

"A tramp turning up where you didn't expect him? Where you thought you were safe?"

"Yes."

"The people who own the Elysian see their hotel as a nice safe investment. A series of vice raids would startle them out of their complacency."

"A series?"

"The police herded two prostitutes out of the Elysian yesterday. It was on TV. In the newspapers."

"Didn't I read that was part of breaking up an escort service?"

"Do you know Catherine Carson?"

"No." Karen flushed under her tan.

"Try again." Congo's tone was skeptical without being unpleasantly so.

"Do you have any sisters?"

He shook his head.

"All girls go through a phase where they dream of sophisticated glamour. When we did our junior high fashion show, one of the mothers brought a video clip of China Doll Carson to show us how it was done. She was my idol. For a while."

"Okay, okay. But I am serious about the dice game. The operator was a not-too-bright wannabe who looked enough like central casting's idea of a gambler to play the role on the evening news."

Karen's eyes filled with mockery. "Oh, you do have an imagination."

"Hillman needs to rattle the owners of the Elysian," he insisted. "To show them they'd better take the deal he's offering. While he's still offering it."

"That owners' group includes some pretty savvy business people."

"People are people. I've been watching them since I was a kid in the carnival. It doesn't take much to scare them into jumping the way you want. A loud noise, a little surprise, anything mildly unpleasant."

Conversation lapsed while the server set out beverages and a salad course. Silence made the restaurant's soft background music conspicuous; an exquisitely rendered piano and violin version of *Will You Love Me Tomorrow*. Congo and Karen caught each other in simultaneous glances and broke eye contact as quickly as two teenagers.

"The gambler's name was Raymond Stepanian," Congo said when the server left. "Ten minutes after I shooed him out of the hotel, he was dead."

Karen became absolutely still, scarcely breathing.

"I'm sorry," Congo said quickly. "I shouldn't have brought that up. Hillman did manage to keep it out of the news."

He reached for the salad dressing and managed to put his sleeve in it. Flustered, he blotted the damp stain with a napkin.

"Do you know how long it's been since I've done that?"

"It's all real, isn't it?"

"What is?"

"Everything you said about your past. It didn't sink in until just now, but you didn't make any of it up, did you?"

"Hey," he said with a boyish grin, "I can do smooth lines as well as the next guy. Seriously. But I think you probably see enough of that. I like you and I want to be straight with you."

She took a bite of her salad. "You're not a natural competitor, are you?"

He moved his shoulders uncomfortably.

"Coming to L.A., buying Crestline. You're looking for sanctuary, not opportunity."

"I'm not about to let anyone take advantage of me."

"But you don't wake up every morning hungry for more."

"Do you?"

"Royce Hillman does."

"It's time he went on a diet."

They ate awhile in silence. Karen checked her cell phone for messages. The server returned and deftly exchanged empty plates for their main courses, hovering to offer condiments. Karen was lively and responsive to the attention.

"What are you going to do?" she asked when they were alone again.

"My best to stabilize Crestline. Before this Athens business comes to a head."

"Let's talk about that."

Between bites of a leisurely dinner, she told him about the prospect she had for the shopping center space they had toured that afternoon. Her cheeks glowed in the candle light but she deflected the personal questions he tried to slip into the conversation. He agreed to meet her and the prospect the next morning at the center.

"I hate to eat and run," she said, "but I want to be home when the boys get back from the game."

Congo stood to help her with the chair. "What do you like to do for fun?"

"I'm afraid motherhood has put my social life on hold for the next few years."

"What do you do when the boys are visiting their dad?"

She touched his arm and gave him a quick smile. "Thanks for dinner."

He grinned sheepishly. "I hope I haven't said anything to chase you away."

"No." Subdued light danced in her hair when she shook her head. "I'll see you tomorrow."

She left without giving any clue why she had invested an evening with a man in whom she denied any social interest and whose business amounted to only a fraction of her visible opportunities.

"Flamingo," Congo said to himself and sat down to wait for the check. His eyes were drawn again to the sparkling city, and to the meandering shoreline where it met the black depths of the ocean, two reservoirs of life, touching but never mingling.

11

Owl-eyed Oscar Reubens was five and a half feet of nervous energy. Wiry and far enough into middle age to look vaguely foolish in jeans and a polo shirt, he paced the corner vacancy in Crestline Center waving forearms as thin as pipe cleaners and matted with the black hair that had abandoned the dome of his head.

"I have to rack ten thousand titles in every location," he told Karen Steele. "I promise that in my ads."

"This space is actually a bit bigger than your Encino store," she pointed out.

"Look what you're giving me to work with."

Emptied of abandoned trade fixtures it was a cavern of ripped carpet and scuffed walls under a random pattern of ceiling fluorescents.

Karen's effervescence never flickered. "It wouldn't make sense for a landlord to put money into the space until he has a signed tenant with firm build-out plans."

Congo held his tongue with the uneasy smile of a man not accustomed to putting his fate in the hands of others.

"You want to talk build out?" Oscar asked. "Okay. Fine. Let's talk build out. I've got to rack folios. I've got to rack CDs. I need a checkout island. And carpet. You know what carpet costs today? Build-out. That's the whole challenge here. I could put a *Used Book Utopia* on every corner in the city if I could raise the cash to build out the raw space."

"What's your estimate?" Karen asked.

"I don't have one. That's the whole problem. If I could get firm estimates, I could get a grip on my sanity. Maybe. To get bids, I need drawings. To get drawings, I need money. Everything costs."

"Oscar," Karen asked in a firm, patient voice, "how can we make this space work for you?"

"And competition. The Internet. They sell used books on line now. I mean, I sign a fixed rate lease, competition cuts my prices, I'm screwed."

"Oscar," Karen persisted, "what's the bottom line?"

"I've got to live here free for a year, minimum, to have any chance to pay back my build-out loan. Percentage only for the rest of the lease. That's the only way it works. I mean, I wouldn't even be here if I weren't looking to move into the Latino market. That's a whole new business for me. I'm going to make beginner's mistakes. There's a learning curve. Any new business, there's a learning curve. I got to factor that into my budget too. I mean, that's it. You talk it over and get back to me."

Nervous energy carried him out the door in strides meant for a taller man. He climbed into a red MGA roadster. With short, wiry Oscar Reubens behind the big British steering wheel, the little car managed to look larger and grander than it was. He started the engine with a puff of blue exhaust from worn valve guides, backed out of the parking stall and motored off with a rising whine from the gearbox.

Congo stood in the open doorway and watched him out of sight. "Does he pull that act with every landlord?"

"I suppose it is partly an act," Karen conceded, "but he is a serious business-man, and a successful one in spite of appearances. Or maybe because of them."

"Is that a polite way of suggesting I should take the deal and be glad of it?"

"You can wait if you want. Perhaps something better will come along tomor-row. I don't know of anything today."

Behind her a nearly empty parking lot was mute testimony to the inertia that gripped the center. Congo's jaw tightened. Even if he hadn't spoken, mental arithmetic would have been obvious on his features.

"If I sign a lease with Oscar, I'll be out of pocket. The water bill is a legal lien on the property. The cost of maintaining the common areas will go up if a new store brings more traffic."

"That same traffic may also shop in the existing stores," she reminded him.

"Do you have any guidance on what that's worth? Rule of thumb or any-thing?"

"There's no magic formula." A sparkle of mischief came to her eyes. "But then, you of all people should know life is a gamble."

Congo winced. "I hope I didn't give you the impression I used to be some cluck on the poker channel."

"What exactly did you do?" she was curious to know.

"Actually life in the gaming industry is pretty mundane," he confessed. "Indi-vidual players may occasionally have substantial money on a roll of the dice or a turn of the cards but for the professionals it's all just arithmetic. Accounting, eco-nomics and probabilities. I spent the last few years setting up tribal casinos. That was more about management headaches than gaming. One thing I learned was to keep operating expenses as low as possible."

"Do you have something in mind, John?"

"Ask Oscar if he'll pay pro-rata common area maintenance and water charges from day one if I extend his free rent period to fifteen months."

"That might work."

"And ask if he'll pay percentage on anything above the gross sales at his best other location. If he's right about start-up difficulties, it won't cost him anything. If he's not, I ought to have some rent."

She opened her day planner and made notes. "Anything else?"

He gave her a sheepish grin. "Sorry. I should be asking you, not telling you. You're the professional here."

"I don't know that I would have thought of that," she confessed and stowed the planner in a shoulder bag. She stole a quick look in the mirror of her compact while he locked the space.

"Well, thanks for listening," he said. "Brokers usually don't want me anywhere in sight while they're with a client."

"There are times when the parties need to develop a sense of where the other is coming from."

"I could use some of that now."

She reprimanded him with a meager smile. "I told you last night that I'm off the market."

"Other mothers have social lives."

"The boys are at an impressionable age. I have to be careful about their role models."

"Reformed sharpshooters need not apply?"

"It's not what you were," she said. "It's what you are."

"Which is?"

"I want the boys to be enthusiastic about the opportunities that come their way. They can't learn that from a cautious man."

"Look, don't get me wrong," Congo said. "It's great that you want the best for your kids. But I know something about boys, okay? I mean, I used to be one. I went through the whole experience. At ten you pick your nose and read comic books and sulk while you do your chores. Twelve is around the age when you stop communicating verbally. Adult role models won't change that. Adults are just not cool. Remember what you thought of your parents?"

"Which is why parents have to take responsibility." She cocked her head to one side, as if surprised that weren't obvious to any adult.

"Karen, even if you could wrap your boys in a cocoon, it wouldn't be good for them. If they're not exposed to the real world, they won't have any immunity when they have to face it on their own."

"I'm not trying to cocoon them," she snapped. A quick smile apologized for her tone. "Just teach them." She touched a forefinger against his chin. "Like you were taught to drive when you turned sixteen."

"My feet reached the pedals when I was fourteen, so that's when I learned. My drivers' ed car was a GMC stake bed. I haven't towed a trailer in decades, but I did so much of it when I was young that I could probably do it now without thinking. Carnival life demanded it, so I did it. Necessity taught me and it will teach your boys. It's the only thing that can."

"Perhaps you still have something to learn from it," she suggested.

"Meaning?"

"You bought Crestline and just hunkered down."

"What should I have done?"

"You haven't joined the Associated Building Owners and Managers."

Congo made a face. "They don't offer enough to justify the dues."

"Or gotten involved in any community activities. That's where you make your business contacts. Royce Hillman has headed several charity drives."

"For the charity? Or the contacts?"

She compressed her smile in disapproval. "Have you been talking to Madison Palmer?"

"I don't think I know him."

Surprise lifted her eyebrows. "He's one of the owners of the Elysian Hotel."

"I'm still looking forward to my first shareholder's meeting."

She dismissed Palmer with a toss of her hair. "Madison's father left him a few shares of this and a few of that and now he's a gadfly at board meetings all over L.A. If management proposes something, he's automatically against it."

"Does he have anything specific against Athens?"

"This is a forty year old spoiled child looking for attention," she warned.

"Do you think he'll be looking for some from me?"

"Apparently he's called some sort of owners' meeting at his home. The larger shareholders know who he is and they aren't expected to attend."

Congo shrugged it off. "People far enough up the social ladder to inherit things don't invite me to their parties."

Karen pressed her key ring and her Lexus lit up and buzzed briefly. "John, I understand what you're going through. I'm no stranger to risk. Many times I've had to sign a note at the bank for money to live on while I waited for commissions on deals I thought would never close. Believe me, I know how nerve racking uncertainty can be."

"I appreciate your help with the vacancies. I'll try to learn the commercial real estate business as fast as I can."

"I don't think slow learning is your problem."

"What is?" Sincerity made the question urgent.

"You've had some bad experiences in your life. You've let them harden you, make you cynical. A negative attitude can be a self-fulfilling prophecy. Good things are a lot more likely to happen if you're positive."

"Give me a little credit," he said. "If I was that negative, I would have bought Treasury Bills instead of Crestline."

"I'm not criticizing you, John. I like you. I want to see you succeed."

She slid in behind the wheel. Congo closed the door.

"You'll call?"

"I'll talk to Oscar. I think we can make *Used Book Utopia* work. As long as you're willing to take a chance."

"I'm willing to take more than one," he said significantly.

She put on her sunglasses to shut him out. He stepped back onto the curb when she started her engine and watched her out of the lot.

"Madison Palmer," he said softly to himself. He grinned and snapped his fingers.

12

A sapphire blue Maserati whipped past Congo on the narrow canyon road that twisted up from the Coast Highway toward Pacific Palisades, its driver oblivious to the granite outcrop and stunted trees that spiked the margins of the asphalt. Congo held his Porsche to a speed that allowed him to glance-read the map display.

Westfield Terrace branched and curled along a ridgeline. Mature plantings screened expensive homes built in a rambling style forty years gone. A few extra vehicles clustered at the address Congo was looking for.

The man who answered the doorbell wore a peach colored silk shirt, white trousers and canvas deck shoes. His tan was deep and even, his pompadour perfect down to the last strand of sandy hair. A couple of inches taller than Congo's six feet, he peered down with pale blue eyes and cleared his throat lightly.

"Yes?" he inquired in a voice as soft as his thirty pound weight advantage.

"Madison Palmer?"

"And you are—?" Palmer hesitated as if on the brink of answering his own question.

"John Congo. I telephoned."

"Ahh, yes. Come in. Do come in."

He stepped back, admitting Congo to an entry flanked by a sunken living room. Books crowded shelves that rose from carpet to cathedral ceiling. Sofas made a conversation square in front of the fireplace. The rest of the room belonged to a grand piano with sheet music open on the trellis. Palmer closed the door and studied Congo.

"Yes, you would have come on board since the last shareholders' meeting."

"Do you know all the other owners?" Congo inquired.

"Oh, yes, yes. Back to prep school in some cases. A couple from Harvard Law."

"Have you sounded them out on the Athens proposal?"

Palmer smiled indulgently. "That is why I convened this evening's meeting."

A glass slider opened to admit a hum of conversation from a back patio. The brunette who stepped in was tanned as deeply as Palmer, statuesque in white shorts and a halter. She closed the door and strutted to the entry, stopping with the contents of her halter an inch from Congo's chest.

"You," she said, and her voice dropped an octave, "are the mysterious Mr. Congo."

"No, Ma'am. I'm the ordinary Mr. Congo."

She let out a tinkling laugh.

Palmer cleared his throat. "Mr. Congo, my wife, Adrienne."

She took one of Congo's hands in both of hers. "I do hope the drive out here wasn't too much of a bore for you."

"I enjoy driving. It gives me a chance to think."

"I detest it myself," Adrienne said, "but Madison insists on living within our means so here we languish in splendid suburban isolation."

Palmer cleared his throat again. "Adrienne, Mr. Congo is here about Royce's proposal for the Elysian."

"Oh, dear." She patted Congo's hand. "Has Madison been flexing his mighty fourteen shares at you?"

"No, Ma'am." Congo freed his hand gently. "I just stopped out to meet the other owners and get their views on the proposal."

"It's Adrienne, darling. By the by, what do your friends call you?"

"John."

"Well, John, the view you need is that when lions like Royce Hillman roar, mere mortals like Madison quake."

A look of long-suffering patience came to her husband. "Adrienne, I'm simply trying to protect—"

"Of course Madison doesn't think of himself as a mere mortal," she went on as if he weren't speaking. "That's what really bothers him. When the movers and shakers move and shake, it becomes clear to all that my poor, dear Madison just isn't one of them."

"Really, Adrienne." Palmer's words leaked out in an exasperated sigh.

"Darling," she said, finally acknowledging that he was present, "you deny the obvious only at the risk of looking ridiculous."

Palmer forced a smile. "Mr. Congo, if you'll come with me, I'll introduce you to the others."

Adrienne took Congo's arm as they walked back through the house. "You really didn't need a coat and tie to come visit us," she cooed. "We're very informal here."

"Late day at the office," Congo said. "A lease on some shopping center space came in at the last minute."

"What did you wear when you were a gambler? I bet you'd look cute in a dinner jacket."

"I gave them all to Goodwill. I'm trying to put my sins behind me."

"You're teasing," she scolded.

"Aren't you?"

"You could always find out."

"Not me. I'm the flint-hearted mercenary type."

"Tell me, John, what is it that you hard drinking professional gamblers drink?"

"A coke would be nice, if you have any."

"What do you put in it?"

"Ice, if it's a hot day."

"Oh, don't be bashful, darling. Booze is the drug of choice in this household. We have every flavor you could possibly imagine."

"Thanks, but I'm driving."

Madison Palmer opened the slider. "Shall we meet the others, Mr. Congo?"

Fewer than a dozen had gathered on a concrete patio at the head of a kidney-shaped swimming pool. Some sat in plastic chairs around a pair of tables shaded by umbrellas. Others stood with drinks in their hands; convivial and close-knit little cliques lost in their own conversations.

"People," Madison Palmer said with a little more volume than he had used in the house. "People, I think we can get started now."

He gave them an apologetic smile for interrupting and cleared his throat again to get the attention of a couple who hadn't got the message.

"I'd like you all to meet John Congo, a recent addition to the owners' group," he said, and began introductions.

Besides Palmer, two were attorneys. Harv Forrest had the bulbous, red-veined nose of an obvious drinker. He sat heavily in his plastic chair and didn't bother to stir his torpid bulk.

"Muh brother owns ninety-one shares," he announced.

The other attorney was small-boned, sharp-featured Paul Clive. He peered closely at Congo, as if trying to read his character in his features. The three other men were participants in family businesses, but none apparently in charge. They greeted Congo cautiously, as if their first instinct was to protect the legacy from strangers. Three of the women were wives, and seemed more interested in Congo's social and marital status. The fourth, austere with straight raven hair, was a shareholder.

"Shall we get things underway?" Palmer suggested.

The group filled all the chairs. Palmer stood to act as chairman. Congo sat on the edge of a padded chaise in a patch of late evening sun. Adrienne sat beside Congo and gave him an icy glass of Cola.

"Careful what you say," she warned under her breath. "Madison has his very own copy of *Roberts Rules of Order.*"

Congo tasted his drink and made a face.

"Jamaican rum," Adrienne whispered. "It'll put hair on your chest. I like my men with hair on their chests. It gives me something to play with while they're playing with me."

"Cut me some slack, Mrs. Palmer."

"Adrienne." She settled back on the chaise to watch the proceedings.

Paul Clive was first to speak. "Madison, how many shares are represented here?"

Red-nosed Harv Forrest said, "Muh brother owns ninety-one." It was an effort. He took a bracing drink from a tall glass. Nobody paid him any attention.

A quick canvass established that Congo's forty-five shares were the largest holding present, with the raven-haired woman's at twenty and the remainder holding somewhere in the teens, save for Forrest, who had nine.

"Less than two hundred, all told," Clive said.

"Muh brother has ninety-one," Harv Forrest repeated.

Congo asked, "Is ninety-one the largest block?"

"Yes," Palmer said. "There are forty-nine shareholders in all. The large blocks are ninety-one, sixty and fifty. Those comprise the Board of Directors. Save for the Crestline interest, the remaining holders have twenty or fewer."

"So Hillman needs to convince a lot of people to win a majority for his proposal."

"At least seventeen, according to my figures," Palmer said. "And that assumes he gets all the large blocks."

"What are his chances?" Congo asked.

Everyone had an opinion on which way the larger owners would move and they all wanted to flaunt any connection they had with the important players. Palmer managed to restore order by alternately clearing his throat and clucking tolerantly at various offenders.

"None of us have actually seen the proposal," Palmer said, "but I think it's becoming clear that we need to petition the Board to appoint a review committee to scrutinize the terms once we have a copy in hand."

The raven-haired woman stood. "I've heard a lot of talk about money," she said in a cool, critical soprano, "but I wonder if we're missing the crux of the

issue. The property that will be taken over by Athens is a trust. The way it is handled will impact the livability of the city. I think we need to know what Royce
Hillman's plans are along those lines. We need to use our influence to nudge him
in the right direction."

Forrest banged down his glass. "Muh brother owns ninety-one shares."

Everybody began talking at once. Madison Palmer cleared his throat furiously.
Forgotten in the swell of conversation, Congo shook his head at the pointless dis-
cord, stood and made his way quietly into the house.

Adrienne reached the front door first and blocked his exit. The banter was
gone. She stood with her arms folded.

"Madison isn't in your league, John."

"My league?"

Her eyes bored into his. "You snatched the Crestline shares away from Royce
Hillman."

"What's this about, Mrs. Palmer?"

"Protecting Madison."

"When I phoned your husband," Congo said, "I made a point of not mentioning my gaming industry background."

"You've spent your life taking advantage of people's weaknesses."

"Where did you hear that?"

"Leave Madison alone."

"The ridiculous flirting," Congo decided, "was to convince your husband he'd
be better off without me around."

"Madison is fragile. His little crusades are very important to him. People toler-
ate him because they think he's harmless. He hates that. He wants desperately to
find a cause where he'll be taken seriously."

"I can't change that," Congo said.

She unfolded her arms. Softness made her voice more urgent than any volume
could have.

"Whatever your game is, leave Madison out of it. Please."

She opened the door to let him out.

The sun was slipping below the horizon as Congo cranked his Porsche to life.
He rolled slowly back toward the canyon road, pressing out Clint Phillips' home
number on his cell phone.

"Did we get the court order to evict that drug pusher from the Coronado?" he
asked when the big man answered.

"I gotta schedule some cops to serve it."

"When?"

"What's the rush?"

"I just met Hillman's opposition. They give new meaning to the term lightweight. We need to get Crestline operating in the black pronto. That low life is the last obstacle to renting the rest of the apartments."

"I'll try to get the cops out there tomorrow."

"Thanks, Phil." Congo put the phone away.

The canyon road was deserted when he turned down from Westfield Terrace. Dusk turned the bordering vegetation into charred shadows spotted with occasional embers of sunset. Headlights appeared in his mirror, grew rapidly brighter and swung out to go by. The car should have come abreast immediately. When it didn't, Congo glanced back. The fore-end of a shotgun protruded from the passenger window of a white Monte Carlo. He jerked his foot off the gas pedal.

Congo's abrupt deceleration sent the Monte Carlo rocketing past. Brake lights blazed. Tires smoked. The white coupe began to slew. Congo came down one gear and fire-walled the accelerator, passing on the driver's side where the passenger would have no shot at him.

Both passenger and driver were African American. Hooded sweatshirts concealed all but broad, blunt young faces. A quick gear change sent Congo's speed skyrocketing. The needle was nearing one hundred thirty when approaching headlights illuminated a curve below. Congo braked hard and narrowly missed an oncoming sedan.

Horns clashed behind him, suggesting the Monte Carlo had come equally close. Headlights returned to Congo's mirror. More lights made an aura in the dusk below. He rounded a corner on skittering tires. A motor home was climbing toward him, overlapping its narrow lane, looming fast in Congo's windshield. He aimed the Porsche at the space between the motor home and the granite outcrop flanking the canyon.

The narrow sports model found enough room going past to keep its tires on asphalt. Ahead lay open road. From behind came the piercing squeal of tires and a noise like a tin can crumpling. No headlights appeared in his mirror. Congo brought the Porsche down to legal speed, shaking as he struggled to herd it the rest of the way down the canyon.

Sirens screamed on the Coast Highway below.

13

The service manager at the Porsche dealership was a perfect blend of Prussian bearing and efficient movement. He raised Congo's Boxster on an inspection lift and peered upward.

"Well, here is the source of your vibration." He snapped on a latex glove and used his forefinger to separate some loose tire tread.

Congo's smile was dubious. "I would like to make sure the suspension hasn't been compromised."

"We will do a full inspection."

The manager led Congo to his office and brought up a work order template on his computer. "Such tire damage," he remarked curiously while he typed, "usually results from a combination of high speed and extreme cornering stress."

"When can I pick up the car?" Congo asked.

The manager suggested that he call back that afternoon. Congo declined a courtesy shuttle to his office and went out to wait for Clint Phillips.

"How bad was it last night?" Phillips said as he pulled away from the curb.

"Did you get that phone number?"

Phillips dug a slip of paper out of his pocket. "Was it the hormones?"

Congo shook his head.

"So what's the point?"

"When you're holding a Chinese straight, all you can do is bluff." Congo used his cell phone.

"Hello." It was a woman's voice, her tongue hovering between the honey to greet a crony and the acid to fend off another telemarketer.

"Good morning, Ma'am. My name is John Congo. I'd like to speak to either Tony or Nicky please."

"Nicky doesn't live here."

"Tony then." Congo winked at a skeptical Clint Phillips while he waited.

"Yeah?"

"Good morning, Tony. John Congo. You have an uncle, or great uncle, named Demirjian, don't you?"

"I'm up to my butt in relatives."

"There's no need to be hostile, Tony. I just want you pass something along for me."

"Yeah? Like what?"

"Tell him I got his message. I want to talk to him. He can call me at my office. If I don't hear from him, he'll get the same kind of greeting card he sent me."

Silence.

"Did you get all that?" Congo asked. "Or was I going a little fast?"

"Uncle Gregory, he don't like threats."

"I don't give a rat's ass what Uncle Gregory doesn't like. Just tell him." Congo cut the connection.

Phillips scowled. "You ought to sell that act to television. What were you trying to do? Out hormone the hormones?"

Congo grinned sheepishly. "When in Rome, do as the Romans do."

"They're liable to set your fucking toga on fire."

Congo made a face and dug a thick document out of his zipper case. Sticky notes left the portion he had read looking like a yellow armadillo. He buried himself in the contents, adding more notes as he read further.

"What is that thing?" Phillips asked when he had parked in the basement garage of Crestline's office building.

Congo put the document away and handed Phillips a letter.

"Athens Incorporated," the big man read as they walked to the elevator, "is pleased to present the enclosed proposal for a direct and equitable exchange of common stock with the owners of the Elysian Hotel. Is this what you were expecting?"

"One hundred sixteen pages of legal hocus pocus and financial mumbo jumbo." Congo pushed the call button.

"A vote of the shareholders will be scheduled in the near future," Phillips read on. "For those wishing to discuss the proposal, a retreat has been scheduled at the exclusive Playa Blanca Lodge."

"Exclusive is right," Congo said. "I had to call three travel agencies before I found someone who'd even heard of the place. You need a pedigree to get a reservation and a yacht or a private plane to reach the lodge."

"No roads?"

"Nothing a tourist would want to drive on. It's to hell and gone down the Gulf of California."

"John, that's fucking Mexico."

The elevator opened. They stepped into an empty car and Congo pressed the button for their floor. Phillips put his nose back into the letter.

"We hope you will be able to join us for two days of informative conferences and recreational activities. Playa Blanca offers swimming, fishing, hunting and horseback riding. Average temperatures blah, blah, blah. Please call Hillman Management to reserve accommodations for the dates of—shit, they're giving us a lousy three days notice. And Eileen gets in tonight."

The elevator opened and they started along the corridor toward Crestline's office suite. "I'll be going alone," Congo said. "I need you and Les here to watch the store."

"You can't go down there by yourself. Suppose these Hillman jokers were behind what happened last night?"

"What would they gain killing me?"

"What would this shark Demirjian gain? You can't pay up if you're dead. And how would he know where to find you? The Hillman crowd"—Phillips opened the office door—"they're the ones who would have known about that meeting you went to."

Muffie stopped in the middle of putting on her customer-friendly smile. "Oh, hi, Mr. Congo." She checked her notes. "The doctor's office called to say you could get your tetanus booster any time this morning."

"Great."

"And the airplane radio place said they could update your GPS database card tomorrow."

"Thanks."

"And I printed off that internet weather forecast and put it on your desk." Worry infiltrated her eyes. "What's a chubasco, anyway?"

"It's a kind of storm." He gave her a reassuring wink.

The two men went into Congo's office. Congo sat down and set the proposal on his desk. Phillips tossed the letter on top of it and tried to get comfortable in one of the visitors' chairs. Normal furniture wasn't made for his height or bulk.

"What's this Mexico shit about, John? How come you have to go down there?"

"One thing I learned as a carnival brat is that you have to stick up for yourself. It doesn't matter how much bigger or stronger the other guy is."

"That ain't what I mean. What I'm saying is why hold a meeting in Mexico? What's wrong with L.A.?"

"Hillman is probably trying to separate the owners from their lawyers and financial advisors long enough to con a majority of them into the deal."

"What is this deal, anyway? I never did get it."

"On the surface it's pretty simple," Congo said. "Hillman forms a company called Athens. Athens trades its stock for ownership interests in the ten major buildings Hillman manages, including the Elysian Hotel. Now Athens owns the buildings and the people who used to own the buildings own Athens."

Phillips spread his huge paws in helpless confusion. "If everyone winds up with the same stuff, why bother?"

"Control," Congo said. "When a company gets big, it's like Enron or World-Com. No one shareholder or group of shareholders has enough say to influence the way the company is run. Legally that's up to the Board of Directors, which Hillman will pack with his toadies."

"What kind of Benjamins are we talking here?"

"I checked the tax values of the buildings Hillman lists on the back of his business card. They total just under two billion."

The big man's jaw sagged and the air left him in a grunt. He stared at Congo in disbelief for a minute before a knowing smile curved his lips.

"Jesus Christ. These deadpan jokes of yours. Sometimes I don't know when you're shitting me. What's the real number?"

"Two billion dollars."

Phillips shook his head. "Two billion dollars is way out of your class."

"I'm not trying to push into the deal. I'm trying to break it up."

"John, it's a private club at the top. I saw it in the NFL. Even the big stars, the guys with the names and the money contracts, they never got to hobnob with the owners."

"Athens isn't social," Congo said. "It's business."

"There's no dividing line. The big shots deal with the people they party with and party with the people they deal with."

"I'm fine with that, as long as they don't do it on my nickel."

"You're not fine," Phillips said. "You're stressed. It's written all over you. You know how you get when that happens."

"Les thinks I'm shrink bait. What do you think?"

"I don't know anything about that psycho shit. All I know is you tense up and start making bad decisions. Like that situation last night. Why don't you call the cops?"

Congo's features hardened. "You know why."

"You don't get it, do you?" Phillips asked. "You really don't get it."

"Get what?"

"Hey, John, I read the morning paper, okay? Two youths injured in street race. Stolen car crashes in canyon. It's lucky the woman driving the motor home was only shaken up."

"What was I supposed to do? Let them kill me?"

"Don't give me that bull. This started because you decided to take out Raymond's crap game yourself, instead of calling the cops on him. Now you think this Demirjian joker is after you. So you're after him."

"Just to warn him off," Congo said.

"What happened to putting the old life behind you?" Phillips asked.

"It's no crime to talk."

"What do you think?" Phillips demanded. "All you have to do to make it all right is put the dice and the cards in the back of some drawer?"

Congo was silent behind a hard stare.

"The straight world has a different set of rules," Phillips said. "A different way of thinking. You've spent your life doing whatever it took to win. But you can't win all the time playing by straight rules. If you're going to make the jump to the straight world, you're going to have to be ready to lose a few. You've got to put all the bad stuff that's happened in your life behind you and get past the fact you're scared shitless of failing and start thinking the way the suckers do. Otherwise you're wasting everyone's time. We might as well go back to doing what we were doing."

A slow grin spread across Congo's face. "Feel better now?"

"Yeah," Phillips said. "I do." His laugh was uncharacteristically nervous. "So, you going to sack me for popping off?"

"You're not the first person who has told me that. And this isn't the first inkling I've had that I screwed up." An idea flickered behind his eyes. "Unless you're telling me you want out?"

The big man fidgeted. "No. Hell, no. We got a good thing going. We always have had. You and me and Les. You can make money where nobody else could grow cactus. Les and I keep you from being blind-sided. Les keeps the books straight and I watch your back. Why trash it?"

Congo eyed him shrewdly. "You told Eileen you're a real estate executive now. You're afraid I'll screw that up for you."

"What about that woman you took to dinner? How far has she got her hooks in you?"

"I struck out. She thinks I'm not upbeat enough."

"Hillman introduced you to her, didn't he? Did she know you were going to the meeting?"

"She told me not to."

Phillips' glare accused Congo of juvenile stupidity.

Congo shrugged it off. "Look on the bright side. Everything that could possibly go wrong has already gone wrong."

The desk telephone buzzed. Congo pressed the speaker button.

"What is it, Muffie?"

"The police are on line one."

14

The interview room in the downtown police high-rise was a claustrophobic cocoon mirrored in a pane of one-way glass. Congo sat composed in a plastic chair, his face betraying neither thought nor emotion.

Yniguez and Debra Long faced him across a table. Debra Long began filling out a printed form.

"Interviewee John NMI Congo," she intoned for the benefit of a video camera hung from the acoustic ceiling. She provided the date, identified herself and Yniguez and gave their badge numbers. "No other persons present."

She looked more comfortable in business attire than Yniguez did, but neither a silk blouse nor a fresh hair-do took the law enforcement edge off her manner. She started down a brief checklist.

"Mr. Congo, are you here voluntarily?"

"I came," Congo said, "because you insisted."

"I need a yes or no response."

"Yes."

"Were you coerced or threatened in any way?"

"It was simpler than arguing."

"Yes or no?"

"No."

"Were any promises made to you?"

"No."

She finished her entries. "Where were you last night, Mr. Congo?"

"Why do you ask?"

Yniguez's voice was a stalking hush. "This is a police interview, Mr. Congo. We'd appreciate your cooperation."

"I'd just like to know what I'm cooperating with," Congo said in the same level tone Debra Long has used to address the video camera. "I haven't been told why I'm here, what my status is or what rights I may or may not have."

"You said you were here voluntarily," Yniguez reminded him.

"That can change," Congo said.

Debra Long tapped her pen on the desk. "At approximately nine PM last night two men were injured in a vehicle collision below Pacific Palisades."

"If you say so."

"The car they were driving was stolen. A loaded shotgun was found inside. One of the men had a sticky note with the make, color and license number of your car."

"I hope they weren't planning to steal it," Congo said.

"We received reports of two cars street racing below the Palisades. This morning you put your Porsche into the shop. It had tire damage consistent with high-speed, high-stress operation."

"Are you accusing me of something?" Congo asked.

Neither officer spoke.

"Because if you are, I'd like to know specifically what it is. And I'd like to call my lawyer."

Yniguez narrowed his eyes. "Are you familiar with the Rolling Sixties Crips?"

"I've never heard of them."

"Then they hired out to kill you?"

"Shouldn't you be talking to them about that?"

"Mr. Congo," Debra Long began, putting her glasses up into her hair, "we know you are involved in a turf war with the Armenian Mafia."

Congo dismissed the idea with a snort.

"We also know," she continued impatiently, "that they blame you for the death of Raymond Stepanian."

Congo looked from one officer to the other. "Does this have something to do with a man named Gregory Demirjian?"

Debra Long replaced her glasses and added to her notes. "In what capacity do you know Mr. Demirjian?"

"I don't."

A triumphant grin spread Yniguez's thin lips. "You," he pointed out, "are the one who brought up his name."

"The fact that I knew his name doesn't mean I know him. Any more than I know George Washington or Ghengis Khan."

"How did you come to know his name?"

"He approached me for money."

"Can you be more specific?"

"He claimed to be Raymond Stepanian's uncle. Said he had loaned his nephew money. Told me the debt was mine now."

"What sort of loan?"

"He didn't go into details."

"What did you say?"

"I asked him for documentation."

"Did he provide any?"

"No."

"Did he threaten you?"

"Not in so many words."

"Did you threaten him?"

"Why would I threaten Demirjian? Or anyone else, for that matter?"

Debra Long took over. "The Elysian Hotel is your turf."

"I own a real estate company that owns a minority interest in the hotel," Congo corrected.

"Which you took over when Catherine Carson subverted a Federal Bankruptcy proceeding on your behalf."

Congo opened his mouth to say something, but clicked it shut without a word.

"We have Catherine Carson's client list," Debra Long informed him.

"You may have physical custody of the list," Congo said, "but the contents are under court seal."

"That seal will not protect you."

"The seal wasn't meant to protect me," Congo said. "It was meant to protect the reputations of people on top of the social and legal pecking order. If I could take cover behind anything I wanted, hypocrisy would be high on my list."

"The actual bankruptcy is in Federal jurisdiction and outside the scope of this investigation."

"Then why bring it up?"

Yniguez spoke up before Debra Long could reply, his voice cool and sardonic. "A minute ago, Mr. Congo, you were complaining that we hadn't advised you of your situation. We respond with facts pertinent to your situation and now you complain about that."

Congo conceded the point with a contrite smile. "Please continue."

"This department has zero tolerance for organized crime," Yniguez said. "That comes straight from the top."

"Is that why you people were piddling away the taxpayers' money on a two bit dice game? Because someone in a corner office wanted Gregory Demirjian for a trophy?"

"Gregory Demirjian tried to have you killed. He is bound to try again."

"Arrest him," Congo suggested.

"We have no evidence."

"If that's true," Congo said, "you're completely incompetent."

That drew hostile stares from both investigators.

"Look at the facts," Congo said. "You people knew about the dice game. You must have known Demirjian was moving gaming equipment into the city. You had plenty of opportunity to lose marked money to his nephew. You had probable cause to subpoena his bank records, tap his phones and who knows what else."

Yniguez said, "All right. Let's talk about that."

"The voluntary portion of this interview is over," Congo said with a glance at the camera. "For the record, I want to leave now. And I want my attorney present at any future interviews, regardless of content or formality."

Debra Long made a few more notes and closed her folder. "For the record, Mr. Congo, have you been threatened in any way during this interview?"

"No."

"Were any promises made to you?"

"No."

"Frankly, Mr. Congo, I advise you to consider a voluntary polygraph examination. If you have nothing to hide, it might help clear you."

Congo stood. "How does this work? Does one of you come with me, or do I find my own way out?"

Yniguez escorted him down to the lobby. "Don't get any ideas about settling the score. We'll be watching."

Congo took a cab back to his office.

"Hi, Muffie. Any messages?"

"The Porsche place called. Your car is ready. Mr. Phillips said call his cell and he'll drive you over."

"Thanks."

"What did the police want?" she asked. Her smile was tentative, ready to back off at the first sign from Congo that she was intruding.

"To put the fear of God in me." He ran a forefinger under his damp collar and grinned. "They did a pretty good job?"

"Are we in trouble?"

"I may be." An idea began to percolate in the depths of his eyes. "How do you feel about this Catherine Carson thing?"

Her jaw tensed and the corners of her mouth turned down. "If they're going to bust her, they ought to bust all the stuffed-shirt men too."

"Would you be willing to get a message to her? Without telling anyone?"

The initial surprise in her expression morphed into intrigue.

"You'll have to use a pay phone," Congo said. "At least five miles from here."

"There's one where I get my groceries."

Congo wrote a number and put several quarters on the reception counter. "No names. Just tell her you are a voice from the beach. The FBI may contact her. It's a fishing expedition. She should decline the interview."

Muffie wrote that.

"And look," Congo said, "if it sounds exciting now, but you get cold feet when the time comes, that's okay. Just drop the whole idea."

Her eyes bridled. "I'm not scared. I had a date with a federal agent once. What a loser. I think he was the reason they put the 'I' in FBI."

Congo grinned, but before he could speak the PBX rang.

Muffie connected, greeted the caller, listened, said, "One minute, please, sir, I'll find him for you," then put the call on hold. "A Mr. Demirjian."

Congo's grin vanished. He went into his office to take the call.

15

Mystic Rain was less a restaurant than a trip back to a forgotten counter-culture. Tattered posters for defunct rock groups covered plaster cracks. A rear door was open to a private patio separated from the sidewalk by a waist-high hedge and hemmed in by the walls of adjoining buildings. Congo seated himself at an umbrella table.

Behind him was a cinder block wall with a mural bleached to ghastly pastels by the brilliant sun peculiar to the People's Republic of Santa Monica. A middle-aged woman in cut-off jeans and a tank top sauntered out with menus under one arm.

"Can I start you off with a beverage, sir?"

"A glass of milk please."

"Are you familiar with our latte selection?"

A flicker of irritation betrayed Congo's nerves. "I think I'm wired enough."

"Oh, we have decaf," she said while she set out menus for each of the four chairs. "That's our 'why bother' list."

"What list is the milk on?"

The server ambled off.

The people who filtered onto the patio to occupy other tables shopped upscale for their threadbare chic and pretended thirty had happened to someone else. The lunch hour rush began to clog the street beyond the hedge. A familiar sedan rolled past. Gregory Demirjian rode in back and his two henchmen in front. The sedan vanished around a corner.

It was the squat, muscular man who appeared at the door from the restaurant. His fighter's shuffle brought him to Congo's table. He sat unbidden in one of the empty chairs, flanking Congo. His posture was stiff and his silence hostile.

"Good morning," Congo said.

"Yeah." The man's voice was husky, like he had been hit in the throat. His face had been hit hard and often. Scar tissue drooped from the corner of one eye.

"My name is John Congo. What's yours?"

"Arthur."

"How long have you worked for Demirjian?"

A small tic developed at the corner of Arthur's battered eye.

"Are the two of you related?" Congo asked.

"Hey, look, I don't know you. I got nothing to say to you. Let's just wait."

"It may be a while. Lunch time parking is a challenge in this neighborhood."

"Whatever it takes."

The server arrived with Congo's milk. She took one look at Arthur and tucked the latte list back under her arm, almost colliding with Demirjian as she retreated inside. Demirjian waddled to the table and took the chair across from Congo. His aromatic presence smothered the salt tang of the nearby Pacific.

"Good afternoon, Mr. Congo."

"Thank you for coming, Mr. Demirjian."

A younger man straddled the chair across from Arthur. He was tall and rangy, dark-featured. Thick black hair and a bushy mustache gave him the look of an east European gangster from the six o-clock news. A paisley shirt and mail order silk-blend sport coat only reinforced the image.

Congo regarded the newcomers pleasantly. "Can I order you anything? Coffee? Tea?"

"Thank you, no," Demirjian said solemnly.

"Who is your friend?" Congo asked. "Or is he a relative? Arthur is the quiet type. He wouldn't say."

"Arthur left school early to pursue a boxing career. He is sensitive about his limited conversational skills. Eddie you have not met."

A smirk twisted Eddie's lips and left his mustache out of kilter. "Arthur and me specialize in what they call nonverbal communication. People understand us real good."

Demirjian spoke in a patronizing wheeze. "To preclude any rash behavior on your part, Mr. Congo, I would like you to understand that both my associates are carrying concealed weapons."

Congo took a leisurely sip of milk. "If you'll look behind you and to your left, you'll see a Cadillac parked at the curb. If you wave, the man behind the wheel will wave back."

Demirjian satisfied himself with a glance. "You would not have a chance to call for help. Eddie is particularly efficient with a knife. And absolutely silent."

The tall man drew a finger slowly across his throat.

"If I go down," Congo said, "so do you. At this range a twelve gauge would clean out all three of you."

Demirjian's smile could not have been smaller. "Please have some respect for my intelligence. You cannot seriously expect me to believe your man would fire a shotgun into a lunch crowd."

"Check his background," Congo said. "Any stray pellets will hit the cinder block behind me."

"Even if I believed this—"

"Send one of your associates to check it out."

Demirjian humored Congo with an economical nod. Eddie slid out of the chair. His legs were just long enough to step over the hedge. While he was gone, Congo offered again to order something for the others. Demirjian declined with a disdainful glance at nearby diners.

"Decadence," he remarked, "is best left to Europeans. Americans never seem to get it right."

"I wouldn't know," Congo said. "I just picked the place for the tactical layout."

Eddie came back and sat down. "It's a steroid in a flak jacket. He showed me a Remington pump under a blanket on the front seat."

Demirjian patted a pudgy hand on the table. "I dislike threats, Mr. Congo. They are not the way to do business."

"Is that why you mentioned that Mutt and Jeff were armed?"

"I do not like to hear that people are looking for me. I was careful to tell you that at our last meeting."

"And I don't like you hiring a couple of gang bangers to use me for target practice."

Demirjian spread his hands in a gesture of helplessness. "I sincerely regret last night's incident but you have been most difficult about our little business. It became necessary to remind you of your vulnerability."

"Vulnerability is a two way street."

Arthur kicked Congo's shin.

Congo winced, forced a smile.

Eddie smirked.

Demirjian spoke slowly, emphatically. "To a man in my business, Mr. Congo, reputation is everything. If I allow myself to be threatened, if I do not collect what you owe me, word will spread. My other collections will suffer. This you must understand."

"I offered to pay you," Congo reminded him.

"You insulted me. I told you in a forthright and honest way how much I had loaned my nephew and you accused me of exaggerating."

"I simply asked you for documentation."

"You made a joke of my efforts to help him find his way in the world."

Congo's smile flickered out. "Spare me the noble patriarch routine. Raymond couldn't find a bus stop. He was just insulation. Asbestos underpants to keep the heat off your backside."

"You killed my nephew. Now you belittle him when could no longer speak in his own defense. Put yourself in my shoes. What am I to do? I ask you."

"Get real, Demirjian. Why would I shoot Raymond?"

"Do you think me a fool?"

"I'm beginning to wonder."

"I am no longer a young man," Demirjian said. "I do not think as quickly as I once did, so I did not immediately connect your trip to the shooting range with the police interview that preceded it."

A sharp frown etched itself into Congo's features. "What are you driving at?"

"When you became a suspect in Raymond's death, you realized police investigation would establish that you had fired a gun recently. The only way to explain the presence of powder residue on your hands was to fire another weapon at a public shooting range before any tests were made."

"If you're going to watch television," Congo said sourly, "you ought to stick to the educational channels."

Demirjian was unmoved, his stare uncompromising.

"If I shot Raymond," Congo said, "I knew it long before the police came around. Why would I wait to cover up the evidence?"

"To be sure you were in fact under suspicion before you took any action that might reveal your complicity."

"The police weren't asking me about Raymond's death. They were talking about organized crime. They used Raymond to suck you into a criminal conspiracy. They were probably counting on his testimony when they prosecuted you."

Worried thoughts made their way into Demirjian's eyes but he put them aside. "Let us focus on the matter at hand, which is your debt to me."

"All right, let's talk about that. A cheap gangster like you"—Congo ran his eyes over Demirjian in a fair imitation of the Armenian's own disdain—"expensive suit, too much jewelry, more cologne than common sense; it's not hard to guess your moves. After you tried to collect from me, you also tried to shake down Raymond's contact at Hillman Management. You threatened to expose him if he didn't repay what you claimed to have loaned Raymond."

Demirjian tugged the sleeves of his suit coat down so that only a hint of gold links showed in the starched cuffs of his shirt. Congo gave him no chance to voice the indignation rising in his face.

"He refused, of course. You couldn't expose him to the police because he'd been working with the police to trap you. But he did offer you a chance to fire a shot across my bow to scare me into paying up."

Demirjian drew and puffed himself up to all the height and bulk he could manage. "This is my reputation we are talking about. With my reputation, I cannot afford to trifle. I must be paid, and paid honorably."

"You're being used by the same man who set you up for the police," Congo shot back. "Why are you protecting him?"

"Twenty thousand dollars, Mr. Congo. And twenty percent interest for each week the balance remains outstanding."

"Give me a name."

"Quickly, please, Mr. Congo, before I am forced to escalate my collection efforts."

Demirjian stood and waddled into the restaurant. Awkward as Arthur's shuffle was, it still got him through the door a step ahead of Demirjian. Eddie stood, watching Congo until the other two were gone.

"I'm going to enjoy this," he said, and left with a long, casual stride.

Congo used a napkin to wipe the sweat from his face. He left money on the table, pushed his way through the hedge and tried not to limp as he walked to the Cadillac.

"What did they do to your leg?" Phillips asked when he had the car under way.

"Drop me at the Del Mar Club."

"They won't let you in. You got no pedigree."

"Royce Hillman has one. He invited me for lunch."

Phillips shot a worried glance at Congo. "Is he planning to feed you, or eat you?"

16

"I'm told the squab is excellent."

Royce Hillman closed the leather-bound menu sounding pleased with his selection; a none-too-subtle hint that Congo could avoid embarrassment by following his lead. Congo surrendered his menu to a formally dressed Latin server.

"I'll have the Mandarin rice and a glass of milk, please."

The server left Hillman and Congo facing each other across a linen-draped table in one of the Del Mar Club's private dining rooms. Taking the place of a window was a vast oil painting of golfers and caddies from the verdant and forgotten Los Angeles of the 1920's, when the gentry ruled and everyone else knew their place. Hillman removed the spectacles he had used to read the menu.

"John, I don't understand your attitude. I've offered you an opportunity to join the city's most influential business people in an investment with limitless potential. Not only do you spurn my generosity, but you criticize the proposal to other Elysian shareholders."

"I had a conversation with China Doll Carson," was all Congo said.

Hillman put the spectacles away. He removed a heavy linen napkin from its silver ring, spread it on his lap and set about buttering a roll, allowing the subject to drift away and lose itself among the shadows under the remote ceiling.

"Tell me, John, what sports did you play in school?"

"I didn't," Congo said.

"No sports?"

"No school."

Disbelief clouded Hillman's features.

"Nothing permanent," Congo corrected. "My mother was a carnival performer. We lived on the road."

"And your father?"

"I never knew. Or wanted to."

"Became a bastard the easy way, did you?" Malicious amusement danced in Hillman's small eyes.

Congo opened a roll, using a table knife deftly and delicately, ignoring the executive as Hillman had ignored him.

"Seriously, John, who was your male role model?"

"Excuse me?" Congo lifted his eyebrows.

"Tell me about the man who had the most profound impact on your life."

Congo took a minute to ponder the question. "The chief accountant at a casino in Tahoe. He took a chance on me when I got out of the service. Gave me a job I wasn't qualified for on faith that I could pick it up."

"John, I'm looking for someone who provided an example of leadership, not charity. Someone strong who—"

"He taught me the basics of risk and finance," Congo went on, buttering his roll as if he weren't aware Hillman had spoken. "Double-entry book keeping. The mathematics of probability. The principle of regression to the mean, which requires that things always average out in the end. The stock market always rises after it falls, and always falls after it rises. No winning streak lasts forever. If it did, one person would wind up with all the money in the world."

Hillman waited to be sure Congo was finished. "All right. Let's talk about your time in the service. Tell me what you learned about leadership and team-work there."

"I learned the athletes who stayed home were treated like gods; while kids who came back from national service with nothing but a thousand yard stare were gar-bage. I resented that at first. Then I got into sports betting. The athletes were just farm animals, pulling the plow until their legs gave out. They bought me my first car and my first good clothes. It all evens out in the end."

"John," Hillman said, suppressing visible exasperation, "I'm trying to make a point here. About some of the things you were exposed to in the service. About—"

"What's your military experience?" Congo asked. "A little ROTC at Yale? A few trips to the Cineplex to watch the Allies invade Normandy again?"

"Don't think just because I didn't serve in some war that I lack resolve. Not all toughness comes from military service."

"War isn't about toughness or resolve. It's just a dirty job dumped off on kids with no options."

"But you had to pull together as team and follow orders to accomplish your mission."

"Cineplex," Congo said sourly. "When you're eighteen years old, ten thou-sand miles from everything you ever knew and drowning in your own sweat, all that matters is keeping yourself and your friends alive."

The server chose that moment to return, wheeling a polished hardwood cart. He came to the table on cat feet and set out salads, garnishing Hillman's to taste before he left. Hillman ladled dressing with practiced efficiency and passed across the silver service.

"Team goals are what matter, John. We all have to learn to put the interests of the group ahead of our own selfish concerns."

"You're getting ahead of yourself," Congo said. "Teamwork isn't used until phase two of the long con. In phase one you're trying to rope the mark. That's when you want to talk up things like positive attitude and leadership. Encourage him to take moronic risks to prove he's got the right stuff. Save teamwork and responsibility for later to keep him from jumping ship when he starts to get an inkling of how dumb he's been. No one wants to think he's slacking or letting other people down."

Hillman's eyes narrowed behind protective pads of fat. "Are you a cynic, John, or just a smart ass?"

"The Athens deal makes no sense. Sooner or later the rental market you're counting on to pay the fat mortgage will go sour on you. Everything averages out over time."

"Athens is the future," Hillman insisted. "And not just of Los Angeles."

"A few stuffed shirts playing an overgrown game of Monopoly aren't going to shake the foundations of civilization."

Hillman returned to his salad. Congo picked at his own, eating the little cubes of garlic bread, smothering the greens in dressing and ignoring the insipid garnish. The server returned with the main course, trading plates, inquiring about beverages, seeing to the diners' needs.

Hillman peered disapprovingly at the pile of rice, stir fried vegetables, shrimp and chicken that covered Congo's plate. He used a knife and fork to cut a bite from his own carefully arranged fare.

"John, if you're not prepared to discuss the Athens project intelligently, why did you come?"

"I don't like being shot at."

Hillman chewed thoughtfully.

Congo attacked his lunch with more gusto than the Del Mar Club was probably accustomed to. "Last night. Coming down from Madison Palmer's place in the Palisades. It turned out to be a scare commissioned by a loan shark named Gregory Demirjian. Raymond Stepanian's uncle. The man who bankrolled Raymond's game in the Elysian Hotel. Feel free to jump in here any time the music moves you."

"I've never met either man," Hillman said.

"Thank you. I wondered whether you handled that sort of thing yourself or left the unpleasant details to Easter."

Hillman's hard stare offered no apology. "The future belongs to men with the courage to seize it. I want you to tell me here and now, man to man, why you can't find the guts to sign on to the Athens deal."

"Let me know when you graduate from junior high school," Congo said. "I'll buy you a root beer float."

"What are you talking about?" Hillman demanded.

"That's the last time I recall hearing 'neener, neener, you're chicken,' as a reason for doing something stupid."

"The men who built Los Angeles faced the same risks we face today," Hillman said. "Their names are now on the major streets and buildings of the city."

"Is that what you really want?" Congo asked. "The elite gathering at the Hillman Center for the Performing Arts? Cars choking the Hillman Freeway every rush hour? The Hillman Peace Prize?"

Hillman finished his lunch, patted his mouth with the linen napkin and dropped it in a wad on the table.

"A bit of history for you, John. Early California had a significant Chinese community. A group isolated by language and culture; beasts of burden originally brought in to work on the railroads. They had no access to the regular workings of law. So when a serious violation was committed by one of their own, punishment was visited by ostracism. Offenders were simply pronounced dead, beyond which point no one in the community would speak to or deal with them. Starvation or suicide came in due course, and made reality of the fiction."

Hillman pushed his chair back, raised his considerable bulk and left Congo to ponder what he had said.

Congo said, "Buffoon," to the empty room and went down to the club's ornate lobby. He settled into a gondola chair and used his cell phone.

"Phil, John."

"How was your fling in high society?"

"I think I've just been flung."

"This is L.A. Mean dogs rule."

"Mean isn't the word for Hillman," Congo said with some concern. "He's got more than one screw loose."

"Then the two of you ought to get along fine," Phillips shot back. "Why don't you just sell him the fucking shares?"

"He won't buy what he thinks he can steal. Are you anywhere near here?"

"I'm due to meet a couple of L.A. County's finest at the Coronado in twenty minutes."

"Swing by and pick me up," Congo instructed.

A few seconds of dead air preceded Phillips' uneasy response. "I don't know, John. You're not exactly Mr. Rapport where the cops are concerned."

"I can be as polite as any square when they're looking out for my interests."

"You're the executive type. You've got better things to do than evict drug dealers."

"Phil, when I want to argue, I'll get married."

17

An Iberian stucco façade made the Coronado Apartments stand out among soulless construction that could have flanked any seedy arterial from San Diego to Seattle. A dry fountain in the forecourt added a forlorn touch of elegance. Phillips parked his Cadillac behind a decrepit Toyota with a door and front clip replaced from different colored wrecks. Congo glanced up and down the street.

"I don't see any Sheriff's people. Are we early?"

"Couple of minutes," Phillips said.

Tension was etched into Congo's face. Restless fingers rippled on his trouser leg. Phillips eyed him warily.

"Hey, John, why don't you sit this one out? Wait in the car. Put on some tunes."

"I'm a landlord now, Phil. Eviction goes with the territory."

The big man let out a derisive snort. "You're just looking for action. You're frustrated because your lunch with that Hillman character didn't go the way you wanted."

"I'm not sure what I wanted," Congo said.

"I don't know why you bothered talking to him."

"It's like they taught you in the NFL, Phil. Always keep your opponent in front of you."

"Horseshit."

"What's eating you?" Congo asked. "Did Eileen break your date?"

Phillips' voice hardened. "She's coming in with some kind of sales team. They're going to a hotel together." He dismissed the possibilities with a helpless shrug. "She's supposed to call me when she's settled."

"Life's like poker, Phil. Sometimes you have to lose a few hands in the early going to win big later."

That only made Phillips sulk. A Sheriff's cruiser rolled by on the street and pulled into a loading zone. The promise of action roused the big man.

"Show time," he said.

He led the way to the cruiser and introduced both of them, giving Congo no opportunity to do anything but smile.

The driver was a middle aged African American who had Congo sign a disclaimer absolving the County of Los Angeles and the Sheriff's Department of liability for any damage, incidental or consequential, to the service of eviction.

The second deputy was younger, big and blond, wearing reflective sunglasses. "Raul Estevez," he read from the paperwork. "Does this guy speak English?"

Phillips grinned. "He was doing pretty good when the LAPD busted him a couple of days ago."

The two officers exchanged surprised glances. The younger man entered Estevez's name into the cruiser's computer.

"Booked into County on possession with intent."

"Bail's always late getting into the system," his older partner said. "This Estevez could already be out and we wouldn't know it."

"No record for assault," the blond deputy said and looked at Phillips. "Any trouble here?"

Phillips moved his massive shoulders in an innocent shrug. "He never tried anything with me."

"No kidding," the older deputy said. "Anybody else live there?"

"He's got an old lady," Phillips said. "I got the master key if there's nobody home."

The two deputies got out of the cruiser adjusting equipment belts and straightening the radio microphones fastened to their epaulets. Armored vests bulked under short-sleeved uniform shirts beginning to stain at the armpits. The four of them started toward the forecourt, past a mother herding two toddlers along the sidewalk in rapid sing-song Spanish.

The blond deputy asked, "Either of you habla Espanol?"

"Muy poquito," Congo said.

"Well if this Estevez's old lady gives us the 'no Engles' routine, you may have to do some explaining. Nobody talks that stuff more poquito than Edgar and me."

Edgar nodded agreement. "Bunch of damn jabber. This part of town, I never know what's going on around me. Gives me the willies sometimes."

As they turned into the forecourt, the front door of the building opened. A short, unlovely woman pushed out clutching a large purse to her ample stomach. Purple ribbons accented tightly braided hair. Stumpy legs in neon green slacks gave her the momentum of a bulldozer.

Phillips said, "That's Estevez's old lady."

The woman saw them and stopped. Her eyes became huge.

"Policia!" she shrieked.

"No Migra!" Congo called out to assure her they were not immigration police. "No Migra!"

She thrust a hand into the purse and brought out a black .22 target automatic. The pistol flashed and snapped at him. He dropped flat behind the concrete skirt surrounding the fountain.

Phillips and the two patrolmen rushed the woman. The rapid-fire pop of the .22 sounded like a string of firecrackers. The shooting ended in a flurry of screaming and cursing. Congo came cautiously to one knee behind the cover of the fountain.

Clint Phillips sat on a stair at the front door of the building. The big man held his midsection. Blood soaked into his shirt and seeped through his fingers. Disbelief covered his face.

The blond officer lay on his back on the walk. He twitched a little and his mouth moved spasmodically, without sound. Blood pooled under his neck and dribbled into a crack in the concrete.

The woman lay face down and squirming on a bit of brown lawn. Edgar stood over her, pinning her wrists behind her with steel cuffs.

He keyed the microphone at his shoulder.

"Officer needs help! Officer down! Shots fired!"

He listened to the dispatcher's response while he trotted to his fallen partner, gave the address and said, "Hurry, damn it!" as he knelt beside the big blond deputy.

Congo came unsteadily to his feet and made his way to Phillips. The initial shock of the big man's wound was passing into pain.

"Son of a bitch luck," Phillips said through clenched teeth. "I pull all kinds of illegal crap with you and never get a scratch. I try to serve a court order with two cops and I get fucking shot."

"Take it easy," Congo said. "The medics are on the way. Do you want to lie down?"

"No. It hurts when I move." A fresh wave of pain swept across his face. "Damn, it hurts."

Congo looked around frantically. Edgar's efforts to administer aid to his partner had come to nothing. The helpless look on his face suggested he had exhausted whatever first responder training he had received. He slipped the younger man's sunglasses into a buttonhole, almost reverently.

"She got a neck artery," he said in a husky whisper, as if he couldn't believe it.

The woman recovered from the surprise of being thrown down. She began screaming in Spanish and struggling to get to her feet. Edgar stood, strode over and kicked her legs out from under her.

The commotion had attracted a crowd. People stood on the sidewalk gawking into the forecourt. More people looked down from open windows in the building. Some of them yelled at Edgar in Spanish. He came to where Congo stood.

"I didn't want to shoot no woman," he said. "He's going to die because I didn't want to shoot no damn woman."

"There was nothing you could do," Congo said. "It happened too fast."

Edgar took the target automatic out of his belt. It was locked open and empty, harmless.

"Goddamn .22," he said. "Goddamn toy."

"Look, I'm sorry," Congo said. "It was just supposed to be a simple eviction."

"How bad are you hit?"

"I'm not."

"Man, that ain't ketchup on your collar."

Congo's hand went to the starched fabric. His fingers came away damp and red. Awareness of the wound brought the first expression of pain, and an irritable curse. The wail of an approaching siren sent Edgar trotting toward the street to hurry help to his partner. Congo fumbled the cell phone from his coat pocket. He pressed the speed dial number for his office.

"Good afternoon. Crestline."

"Muffie," Congo began in a shaken voice, "is Mr. Lester there?"

"Yes, sir." A quick response that sensed the trouble in his tone.

"John?" Abe Lester asked worriedly.

"Phil's been shot."

"What?"

"There wasn't a damned thing I could do."

"Where are you?"

"At the Coronado. We came to serve the eviction order on Estevez."

"The drug dealer? Phil said the narco squad popped him. He's supposed to be in the County bucket."

"His old lady opened up on us with a .22. Phil took a round in the gut."

"I thought the cops were supposed to be there."

"One of them was hit, too." Congo glanced at paramedics running toward the fallen deputy. "I don't think he's going to make it."

"Jesus H. Christ."

Phillips hunched over, moaning. Patrol cruisers massed out on the street. More paramedic teams arrived.

"Hang on, Phil."

"Jesus. It hadda happen on the day Eileen is getting in."

Congo patted his shoulder. "Don't worry about that. We'll get word to Eileen."

"What's she gonna think?"

"I'll explain it to her," Congo promised. "I'll make time to talk to her before I leave for Mexico."

Phillips caught Congo's arm, his grip a shadow of his normal strength. "Don't go, John. Those goddamn suits are playing for keeps. You won't come back."

"John!" Lester yelled over the phone.

One paramedic team swarmed over Congo, sitting him on the stairs, putting a light into his eyes, taking his pulse, opening an impact case, unrolling a blood pressure cuff.

"Relax, Sir," one said as they pulled one arm out of his coat to get the cuff around it.

"John!" Lester yelled again. "What the hell's going on?"

"Goddamn paramedics," Congo said.

"John, were you hit?"

"One forty over ninety five," one technician announced.

"He'll pump himself dry. Normal saline."

The technician ripped an IV out of its protective cover while his partner signaled an approaching gurney to hurry.

Congo squirmed. "I'm okay. I can walk."

"Sir, you need to relax. You need to bring your heart rate down."

One paramedic, two ambulance attendants and a police officer lifted Congo bodily and strapped him onto the gurney while the other paramedic tried to pry the cell phone from his fingers.

"Look, Les, I won't be able to ride the ambulance with Phil. They'll probably take him to White Memorial. Take the health insurance documentation with you. Make sure the hospital understands that Crestline will pay for anything he needs that's not in the package."

"Right. Yeah. I'm on my way."

Congo gave up his struggle for the phone. A needle went into his arm and a paramedic taped it down. Brilliant California sun made shimmering patterns through the swaying IV bag as the gurney started to move.

18

Congo opened his eyes, squinting against brilliant light. He lay on his back on a narrow bed in an O.R. gown. A petite Korean woman stood over him. A stethoscope hung around her neck. A photo ID badge clipped to the pocket of her hospital coat identified her as a resident.

"Remember me?" She opened a metal chart holder.

"Just your eyes," he said. "That was all I could see, except for the surgical costume and the Frankenstein glasses."

"How are you feeling?" She took his wrist to check his pulse.

"Not as bad as I expect to when the anesthetic wears off."

She made an entry on the chart. He fingered the dressing on the side of his neck.

"What did you find?"

Her smile was full of reassurance. "From the amount of color under the skin, we were afraid there might have been some venus trauma, but it turned out that the bullet transected a capillary-rich region and produced abnormal seepage."

She produced a penlight and shone it into one of Congo's eyes then the other.

"It did nick a tendon," she went on, "so that neck will hurt for a while. I'll see that you get a prescription for something that will ease the pain." She made another note. "I'll schedule you back in a week or so to have those sutures out and we'll do an evaluation then."

"Am I done for now?" he asked.

"You should limit your movements for another hour. There are two gentlemen who would like to talk to you. I'll look in when you're finished."

She left and two Sheriff's detectives came in. The badges they displayed had black mourning tape across them. Congo brought himself to the best sitting position he could manage on the narrow bed.

The smaller detective was middle-aged and buttoned-down, with gray hair cut short. The little curtained-off enclosure had no chairs, so he had to sit on the foot of the bed to open a computer on his lap.

The interviewing officer remained standing. A ponderous belly in a blue shirt pushed its way out of his open sport coat and a garish tie cascaded down from a rumpled collar.

"Mr. Congo," he began in a patient rumble, "I understand you have had recent contact with the Organized Crime Intelligence Unit of the Los Angeles Police Department?"

Congo blinked in confusion. "I don't know," he realized. "I mean, yes, I talked to the police, but they didn't say specifically what they did."

"Were this afternoon's events at the Coronado Apartments connected in any way with events under investigation by the Los Angeles Police?"

"No. That was a court ordered eviction. The action was filed weeks ago."

"You're sure?"

"It's a matter of record," Congo said.

"All right, sir. Let's go over what you saw and what you did."

The soporific rhythm of questions and details could not mask the enormity of what had happened at the Coronado; only reduce its startling speed to an excruciating stop motion as each movement was minutely dissected. Congo's slow and sometimes halting answers betrayed the presence of anesthetic still in his system. The odors of medical practice infiltrated and asserted themselves. Congo's face paled and he began to perspire.

"Are you going to be all right, sir?" the investigator asked.

"I don't know."

"Would you like to take a break?"

"Is there some way we can check on Clint Phillips?"

"I'm sure the medical staff is doing everything possible, sir."

"Let's get this over with."

The investigators would not be rushed. Another hour passed before they exhausted their questions.

"We'll have your statement printed for signature," the larger man said.

The other officer closed his laptop and the two of them left. Congo sagged back on the bed. Time passed. Voices drifted beyond the curtains. One was familiar. Debra Long came in. She wore jeans and a denim jacket over a denim shirt. Her hair was pulled back in a tight pony tail. She was alone.

Congo forced himself to sit up again. "I thought you people traveled in pairs. Like nuns."

"Mr. Congo," she began tartly, "I suggest—"

The Sheriff's investigator pushed his big blue belly into the curtained enclosure.

"Excuse me, Ms. Long. The Captain wants to see this paperwork right away."

She moved only enough to allow the investigator to hand Congo his printed statement. Congo absorbed himself in reading.

Debra Long asked, "What is Mr. Congo's status?"

"Status?" the investigator asked.

"We were notified that a Sheriff's deputy had been fatally shot."

"Mr. Congo was a witness. We notified OCIU only because you posted a standing request to report any police contact associated with his name."

Congo initialed each page of the statement top and bottom and signed the last. The investigator took the statement, thanked Congo and excused himself.

Congo stood to confront Debra Long. Blood drained and left his face ashen. His balance was none too steady. He had to moisten his lips to speak.

"Organized Crime Intelligence Unit," he said. "Is that what OCIU stands for?"

"Yes."

Congo massaged the bridge of his nose. "What happens to your career if you don't find any?"

"What are you implying?" she asked.

"If the police think I killed Raymond Stepanian, why haven't I been interviewed by homicide investigators?"

"Are you suggesting some breach of procedure?"

"Just the opposite," Congo said. "The police are required by law to investigate Raymond's death. The only thing that could end that investigation is closure. Since no arrests have been made, it's a safe bet the investigation found nothing that would support a criminal filing."

"Mr. Stepanian's death," she said, "is peripheral to an overall organized crime investigation."

"Do you think I'm completely stupid?" Congo asked.

She said nothing, regarding him with shrewd eyes, waiting for him to vent his irritation.

He sat back on the bed.

"You learned Stepanian was romancing a Hillman employee named Rachel Krebs trying to get a foot in the door at the Elysian," he said. "You prevailed on Hillman to let him in. You knew Uncle Gregory would take over to make sure Raymond didn't screw up a golden opportunity. Demirjian would trap himself in a gambling conspiracy and Stepanian would testify against him. But Stepanian wound up dead and left you with egg on your faces. Instead of fessing up that you had blown several thousand dollars worth of investigative budget, you told your supervisors you had uncovered some kind of gang war."

"Was the conspiracy to obtain an interest in the Elysian Hotel limited to you and Catherine Carson?" she asked. "Or were others involved?"

Weariness settled visibly into Congo's posture and dulled his voice. "I've never been involved with organized crime. They wouldn't have any use for me. No organization would. I'm a loose cannon."

"You came to Los Angeles after several years of setting up casinos on any plot of land that could remotely be construed as Native American Reservation."

"I came here to put that behind me," he said.

"What happened? Did you run out of reservations? Or did the tribal lawyers just get too smart for you?"

Congo shivered and used a sleeve to mop perspiration from his face.

Debra Long did not relent.

"A police officer has been killed removing a known drug dealer from a building owned by you."

"The drug dealer was already in jail," Congo said. "He was arrested yesterday. Three of us, myself included, were shot by a terrified woman for reasons I could only guess at."

"That's the second time you've been shot at. For an honest man, you attract a lot of gunfire."

"This conversation is getting redundant. If you'll excuse me, I have pressing business to attend to."

"Do you know what a material witness is?"

"Unfortunately, I do. It's a special status that can be conferred only by the Superior Court in this state. Do you have a court order?"

"You are not to leave Los Angeles," Debra Long said. "You are to make yourself available for interview as required."

"No more interviews," Congo said. "If you have charges, file them. Otherwise, leave me alone."

They stared at each other. She left him with another warning not to leave Los Angeles. He made a nuisance of himself at the nursing station and was allowed to sign for his clothing and personal effects.

The nurse had no information on Clint Phillips. When Congo persisted, a supervisor explained that Federal privacy laws would forbid disclosing Phillips' condition even if they could obtain it. The petite Korean resident returned while he was dressing.

"Well, you seem to be recovering nicely," she said after a quick pulse check.

"I'd be surer of that if the rest of the world would stabilize."

"A little wooziness is normal after traumatic blood loss. Drink plenty of fluids. Eat balanced meals. Give your body a chance to re-build electrolytes."

"Will I be able to fly tomorrow?"

"I don't see why not. If you feel light-headed, just ask the cabin attendant for a salt tablet."

"I'm sorry. I wasn't clear. I meant a personal airplane. Light twin engine."

She smiled indulgently. "I don't specialize in aviation medicine, but I do suggest postponing any strenuous recreation until you feel a hundred percent."

"There's nothing remotely recreational about this trip."

19

Heat flowed in shimmering waves across the runway at Mexicali airport, rocking the wings of Congo's twin engine Beechcraft Duchess as he bled off the last of his airspeed prior to touchdown. He rode out a bumpy arrival and radioed ground control for taxi instructions to Customs.

Mexicali was a main clearance point and officers had inspection, forms and fees down to a polite, tedious routine. When they were done, Congo telephoned air traffic control.

"Welcome to Mexico, Mr. Congo. We have received your flight plan. There is a severe weather advisory for the southern leg of your trip."

"Just an advisory?" Congo asked. "Not a warning?"

"Not at this time, sir. Do you wish to revise your flight plan?"

Congo worried his lower lip between his teeth. "No," he decided. "Thank you."

"You are clear as filed to Playa Blanca Lodge. Have a pleasant trip."

Congo lost no time getting airborne again. The temperature eased as he climbed. He leveled off two miles up, where he could run smoothly and economically without perspiring in the subtropical sun.

The Duchess was a hand-me-down, bought cheaply when a flying school went out of business, the airframe past its twenty fifth year, the engines rebuilt one at a time when finances permitted, the radios replaced by modern avionics as bargains appeared, the maroon and white paint finally refreshed only months ago. Congo clicked on the single-axis autopilot and let it follow the radio signal guiding him down the eastern coast of the Baja peninsula.

Beneath his right wing the desolate landscape of Lower California scrolled out endlessly. Mountains in places, and the great inland desert as featureless as the parchment maps of the Conquistadors. The engines droned and time drifted past. There was no air traffic control radar in Mexico, so the blips of light from his transponder meant that U.S drug enforcement was tracking him.

Clouds appeared on the horizon, the foothills of an approaching storm. The autopilot moved the nose gradually in response to a rising crosswind that tried to push the Beechcraft off course. The ground speed shown on the satellite navigation readout fell gradually and stabilized thirty miles an hour below the reading on the airspeed indicator. The plane shuddered momentarily at a wave of turbulence. Congo called air traffic control and gave his position.

"I have towering cumulus to the south," he said. "Has the severe weather advisory been updated?"

"No, sir. A tropical depression continues to track toward Southern Baja."

"Any coastal storm reports?" Congo asked.

"Not at this time, sir. Do you wish to turn back?"

"Negative," Congo decided. He stowed his loose navigation charts, cinched his shoulder harness and disconnected the autopilot.

Clouds rose up and closed in. Rain rattled against the airplane's metal skin. Night could not have been any darker. Unable to see the horizon, Congo had to constantly scan half a dozen instruments and correct immediately for any variation to keep the plane right side up and on course.

A downdraft dropped the Duchess five hundred feet. He pushed the throttles to full power to climb back to his altitude. Half an hour of violent pitching and intense concentration left him sweat-soaked and pale when a navigation radio came alive with his destination. He keyed the microphone and gave air traffic control his call sign.

"Ten north of Playa Blanca," he said, approximating his position. "Request landing clearance."

"Playa Blanca reports wind four two knots gusting to five eight," came through his headset, broken by static. "Do you want to hold at the beacon until the storm front passes?"

Congo glanced at the wildly flickering needles of his gas gauges. "Not possible. Limited fuel. Request landing clearance."

"Descend to two thousand eight hundred. Fly direct to Playa Blanca. Cleared for the radio beacon approach. Contact Playa Blanca at beacon inbound."

Congo read back the clearance and reduced power to begin his descent.

The turbulence came in layers as he lost altitude, abating briefly then attacking the Duchess with renewed fury. Fluctuating up and down drafts varied his vertical speed between two hundred feet per minute of climb and fifteen hundred feet per minute of descent, with no change in his control inputs. He was in the pilot's seat, but the weather was in charge.

The needle that indicated the direction to the radio beacon wavered and then reversed abruptly as he passed over. Congo switched his radio frequency. His voice could have been steadier.

"Playa Blanca Unicom, Duchess Two One Tango. Beacon inbound for landing. Request airport advisory."

"This is Playa Blanca," came the urgent, Latin-inflected reply. "Hazardous conditions. Suggest you divert to alternate."

"Two One Tango has limited fuel."

The Latin voice came back taut with concern. "We are landing runway one four today. Wind niner zero at four two, gusting five zero. Estimated ceiling six hundred. Visibility one mile in heavy rain."

Congo peered ahead into the unbroken blackness. "Two One Tango. Request field lights."

"The field lights are on."

Congo's altimeter jerked erratically downward—seven hundred feet, six hundred, five hundred fifty. He broke through the base of the clouds into black scud drifting in the downpour. Lightning ripped the sodden sky and showed a cluster of low buildings huddled along a wave-lashed shoreline. Lights marked the airfield beyond. Congo herded the Duchess toward them.

The ground reflected and magnified the turbulence. The last of the buildings passed under his bouncing wings. He pushed the propellers to full advance in case he had to go around for another try. Next came the landing gear switch and the nervous glances until green lights verified that the wheels were down and locked.

Asphalt appeared in the frame of the field lights and rose to meet him. The head wind meant his seventy knot air speed translated to only about forty knots of ground speed but the powerful cross wind was beyond the limits of his rudder to correct for. He would have to land with the plane crabbed sideways. Runway numbers drifted beneath the wings. He struggled to keep the Duchess over the center line.

The tires bit asphalt, shuddering and sliding on the wet surface. Congo cut power instantly and retracted the flaps to keep any stray wind gust from sending the Duchess airborne again. The plane's speed bled away and he turned off onto the taxi way, shaking and visibly drained.

The field had a large hangar with several expensive multi-engine aircraft chained down on the asphalt in front. A young Mexican in a billowing yellow slicker guided the Duchess over a tie-down tee. Congo cut the engines and climbed out on wobbly legs to help the youth chain the shuddering plane against the gale.

He was soaked to the skin by the time the two of them carried his luggage into the hangar.

A Latin gentleman of forty something waited in an office there. Brief exposure to the downpour had darkened his tan raincoat only across the shoulders. Practice made his smile friendly without being intrusive. He held a wide brimmed hat in one plump hand and extended the other.

"Welcome to Playa Blanca Lodge, Mr. Congo. My name is Pedro Segura. I am the manager. I hope we can make your stay enjoyable."

"Thank you." Congo put his wet hand into Segura's.

A gust of wind-driven rain machine-gunned the hangar.

"Your business must be important for you to fly in this weather." Segura's heavy-lidded brown eyes made the statement a polite question.

"I made a bad decision," Congo admitted in a voice that feared it might be an omen.

Segura helped carry Congo's bags out to a white jeep station wagon with a discreet hotel logo on the door.

"Is it normal for the manager of the hotel to drive down to pick up guests?" Congo asked as Segura got the jeep underway.

"I thought you and I might both benefit from a short talk."

"Meaning you have a copy of the Nevada Black Book."

"I have nothing personal against professional gamblers. In my romantic youth, I even imagined becoming one. But I do have a responsibility to my guests."

"I was born on the gypsy carnival circuit," Congo explained. "Gaming was part of the culture. I went with the flow until I made enough money to put it behind me."

"How does this bring you to Playa Blanca?"

"I'm here for a business conference, Mr. Segura. I'm not here to make trouble."

Segura's smile was as thin as the mustache that traced his upper lip. He turned the Jeep along a road paralleling the beach, where waves crashed against a sea wall and threw spray up over the pavement.

"That angry water is called the Gulf of California. When my father first brought me to this shore it was called the Sea of Cortez and we were proud that the blood of the Conquistadors coursed through our veins. Today such sentiment is no longer politically correct. The water has not changed. Only the men who gaze in wonderment at its majesty."

"Meaning I'm the same chiseler I always was?"

"You are, of course, welcome as a guest. As manager I am here to assist you."

Segura stopped the Jeep, took one of Congo's bags and led the way along a flagstone path that wound among low bungalows with cantilevered roofs and large picture windows.

"Fortunately Mr. Hillman made reservations several weeks in advance," he said, unlocking one and letting Congo in. "We were able to provide some beach outlook for almost everyone in the party."

"It would have been nice if Mr. Hillman could have given the owners the same notice," Congo remarked.

A crackle of Spanish came from a radio in Segura's coat pocket. He informed Congo that the Hillman party was expected for dinner at seven in the main banquet room and excused himself to attend to other business. Congo picked up the telephone and began to unfasten his wet clothing while the hotel switchboard placed a call for him.

"Crestline Properties." Muffie's voice, distant and distracted.

"It's me. Can I speak to Mr. Lester, please?"

"He's not here, Mr. Congo. He had to go to the hospital. Mr. Phillips died." All that in a sudden burst.

"What?" Congo gripped the phone, his knuckles white.

"The hospital called about an hour ago."

"They had him stabilized," Congo protested. "He was supposed to come out of intensive care today or tomorrow."

"I guess the internal bleeding started again and they couldn't get it stopped."

Congo sagged into a chair. "How are you holding up?"

"I'm okay. Except it just doesn't seem fair."

"We play the cards we're dealt," he said in a hollow voice, staring out at the storm that might have killed him. "We don't control when the game ends."

"When are you coming back?"

"When I've done what I came to do."

20

Congo showered and sat alone afterward, ignoring telephone, computer, anything that might connect him with the world outside the bungalow; staring at the wind-driven rain that clawed at the windows and flowed down the glass in waves, like gelatin.

After a time the rain eased and the wind picked up, blowing the last of the storm front through. Sunlight poured in the windows only to be blotted out by a straggle of overcast and then creep back in as the clouds scudded away after the retreating depression. Unpacked and dressed by six-forty-five, Congo locked up and set off to find the banquet facility.

Steam rose from lush greenery and decorative boulders. Placid waves rolled in from the Gulf. Campesino labor was already clearing away the broken vegetation that littered the white sand beach. Congo followed a stone path that wound among a maze of bungalows toward a hum of music and conversation.

The path issued out onto a crowded patio. Under the protective overhang of a flat roof one wall of a building was open to permit circulation between the patio and a lounge inside. Pat Easter emerged in a short-sleeved floral shirt.

"John!" He smiled and extended a hand. "I'm glad you could come."

"Thank you."

"Segura told me you flew your own plane down?" Easter's tone suggested a breach of hospitality.

"With more notice," Congo said, "I might have been able to rearrange my schedule to make your charter flight."

"Well, we're certainly happy to have you with us."

"Where is your dinner?"

"Straight through the bar." Easter handed Congo a chit. "You can pick up a drink on your way. Just go on in and mingle. Royce wants to get started at seven sharp."

The bar was less a room than a wide spot in the resort's circulation pattern. An archway hewn from native timber fronted the banquet hall. A Mexican hostess checked Congo's name off a list, made him a calligraphic tag and gave him his table assignment.

Six tables were set to accommodate ten diners each. The guests were gathered in chatty groups at an expanse of windows overlooking a protected cove. Private yachts lay at anchor just beyond the dock where the lodge's sport fishing boats were moored. Motorized drapes began to move, slowly cutting off the view. Silverware made noise against a water glass. Royce Hillman's peremptory baritone carried over the buzz of conversation.

"If we could all move to our tables, we can sample some marvelous cuisine and begin our journey."

Congo's table assignment put him under Pat Easter's watchful eye. The only stranger in a well-acquainted group, Congo was convivial and attentive throughout the formal Mexican dinner, listening carefully but never prying, parrying questions directed at him with smiles and vague answers.

A repeated clink of metal on glass silenced conversation. Several tables away, Royce Hillman rose in a garish Hawaiian shirt.

"I would like to welcome all of you to the first look at the exciting and innovative way real estate will be owned and managed in the coming years. For the next two days we all will be challenged to think out of the box. To let our creative juices flow."

Hillman went on for twenty minutes, rambling through a laundry list of clichés before he surrendered the floor.

Pat Easter stood and detailed a program which included a conference the next day, with various social activities for spouses who didn't want to attend. The final day was given over to hunting, horseback riding and fishing. Each activity would be led by one of the officers selected to manage the new Athens firm.

After dinner the tables broke up into cliques.

Congo was on his way out when Hillman blocked him at the archway, out of earshot of the others. Liquor had begun to inflame the executive's face, but his voice was hard and sober.

"John, this deal is going through. Do you have any questions about that?"

"Do you mind a question that's not connected with Athens?"

Hillman shrugged.

"How was Raymond Stepanian killed?"

The executive's eyes narrowed. "Why ask me?"

"There was no homicide investigation. That means you got to the police with a convincing story."

Hillman smiled. "Anything can be arranged. If you know the right people."

He went back to the party.

Congo went out to the bar and used his chit for a Cuba Libre. He chewed morosely on ceviche, hors d'ouvers of raw fish soaked in lemon juice. The day had left him too drained to make anything of his desultory conversation with a woman on the next stool. He trudged back to his bungalow and placed a telephone call.

"Hi, Les. Sorry if I got you out of bed."

"Late movie on cable," Lester said. "I tried sleeping but it wasn't working out."

"I guess we'll all have some bad nights," Congo said. "Is everything else under control?"

"Yeah. I guess. Shitload of paperwork to do. How about you? That Hillman character given you any grief yet?"

"Not yet," Congo said, "but the party has just started."

Lester's voice was dubious. "This is Hillman's game, John, not yours. He's had a lot more practice than you have."

"Get some sleep, Les. I'll check in with you tomorrow."

Congo hung up, undressed and fell into bed.

Painfully bright tropical sun and eighty degree heat announced the next morning.

The lodge's conference facility was state of the art. A massive projector hung from the ceiling. A slide of the Athens logo filled a white board. Congo collected croissants and juice from a buffet in back. He made a point of socializing with those at his table.

Pat Easter activated the podium microphone. "Good morning, everyone, and welcome to an exclusive preview of the Athens concept. The future of commercial real estate ownership and management."

Easter talked enthusiastically through a brief series of slides that made up the conference agenda, and then introduced an industrial psychologist retained as facilitator.

A skilled speaker in his late thirties, the facilitator quickly engaged his audience by administering a written psychological profile. Congo completed his reluctantly, as if each answer drove another chink into his personal armor.

The results grouped the audience into four personality types—*persuading, analyzing, organizing* or *controlling*. Congo's test score placed him firmly in the controlling group, slightly to the right of Attila the Hun.

Each group was asked to come up with a list of pros and cons for the Athens proposal.

Persuaders (14 people)

Pro: 1. Ahead of the competition

          2. Opportunity for leadership

          3. Size is power.

Con: 1. Dilutes the influence of the Elysian owners

Analyzers (4 people)

Pro: 1. Economy of scale

          2. Diversification of risk

Con: 1. Vague financial projections

          2. Not enough time to consider all facets.

Organizers (17 People)

Pro: 1. Broad ownership perspective

          2. Safety in numbers

Con: 1. Large and impersonal

          2. No input solicited from Elysian owners

Controllers (13 People)

Pro: 1. Growth potential

Con: 1. Restriction on sale of shares

          2. No control over dividends

          3. No control over selection of acquisitions

"I think we can all see," the facilitator said, "that how we feel about the proposal depends as much on what kind of people we are as on the proposal itself. When we come back from lunch, we'll talk about the proposal and how we can reconcile it with our unique approaches to life."

The morning session broke up in excited chatter. People left for lunch clutching colorful booklets that explained their personality type and offered hints for getting along with other types.

Congo made a quick trip to his bungalow.

"Les, it's John," he said as soon as he had a phone connection. "Got a pencil?"

"Yeah. Don't they have e-mail down there?"

"I need a quick turnaround on this, Les."

"You sound stressed."

"Hillman pulled a rabbit out of his hat this morning."

A resigned sigh came across the line. "John, you're out of your league."

"Don't be melodramatic. I just need information."

"What happened?"

"The morning session was run by an industrial shrink, Arvid Ashfeld, PhD." Congo spelled the name.

"He should have gone with Aaron Aardvark," Lester remarked, "and gotten a jump on the rest of the phone book."

"Call Walter Byner. Find out if Hillman has ever used Ashfeld before, and if he has how the guy works."

"You sound sure that he has."

"This morning's program went too smoothly to be a first try," Congo said. "There was a routine to it. I think it came from one of those teamwork seminars. Motivating the drudges to overcome their personal shortcomings and pull together to reach management's goals without getting paid any more."

"Anything specific I should ask about?"

"They're playing a mind game, trying to convince the owners that any objections they have to the Athens deal come from their own psychological make-up, not from any fundamental flaws in the proposal. Byner called it management by psychobabble."

"Is that what has you stressed?" Lester asked. "Are you afraid they may find out too much about your psychological make-up?"

Congo checked his watch. "I'll call you back in an hour, just before we start the afternoon session."

"John," Lester said quickly, before Congo could hang up. "We're burying Phil in three days."

Sadness emptied Congo's lungs. "I should be back late tomorrow."

"Eileen wants to talk to you, John."

"You'll just have to deal with her," Congo said impatiently.

"I don't think I can give her what she wants."

"What's she looking for?"

"Her second marriage never got past the first ring."

"What's that got to do with me?"

"Her bank account's low and her biological clock is ticking."

"Jesus Christ. The last thing I need is a gold digging perfume ninja on my case."

"Good luck," Lester said sourly.

"If she shows up again, warn her about my background. Tell her the police think I'm in organized crime."

"That's the other problem," Lester said. "The cops found out you left the country. They're pissed. They're talking about issuing a warrant."

"Only a court can do that. The police can't issue toilet paper."

"Try telling them that."

"If they call again, give them my lawyer's name."

"John, the cops aren't playing games."

Congo checked his watch. "I've got to go. I don't want to miss the conference lunch. It's my only chance to take the temperature of the other players before the afternoon session. I'll call you back in an hour."

21

Hundred ten degree heat had Congo perspiring by the time he reached the air-conditioned main building. He paused at the entrance to the dining room to pat dampness from his face.

Pedro Segura appeared, cool and smiling. "Mr. Congo, I wonder if I might ask a favor of you."

Congo glanced at a lunch already in progress. "Can I get back to you?"

"The favor would be done this evening. After your conference activities are complete. I hoped to catch you before you scheduled anything."

"What do you want, Mr. Segura?"

"The lodge has a private card room. Many of our guests enjoy a game of poker in the evening."

"Okay." Congo managed a grin. "Tell me where the room is. I won't go near it. Not even to kibitz."

"In fact, I would like you to play."

Congo's grin vanished. "Yesterday you were worried I'd come to fleece your guests. Now you're steering me into a card game with them?"

"I do not imagine that all the professional gamblers who come to Mexico have their picture in what you call the Nevada Black Book. I would like to have you sit in on the game to see if we have attracted any parasites."

"Set a thief to catch a thief?"

"I don't mean to be indelicate."

"Anyone I can spot by playing," Congo said, "I can spot by watching."

"Watching is obvious. I would prefer to be discreet. The lodge will stake you. $2,000 American. You will be charged for no losses. You may keep anything you win."

Congo threw an impatient glance into the dining room. "All right. I'll see what I can do."

"Thank you." Segura excused himself.

Congo went into the dining room and found a seat. Table conversation centered on the morning's personality test results.

"Royce has come up with a refreshing approach, don't you think?"

"Certainly better than the dry sets of numbers we usually have to suffer through."

"And no Power Point to put us to sleep."

Congo limited himself to small talk and returned to his bungalow as soon as he finished eating to call Los Angeles.

"Les, what have you got for me?"

"Byner says that kind of psychological mumbo jumbo went on all the time at Hillman."

"What did you get from the owners of the other buildings that are supposed to be bundled into Athens?"

"Strictly no comment," Lester said.

"Did you press them?"

"Press them how? All I could do was call up and say I represented shares of the Elysian and were they going along with the Athens proposal, blah, blah. A couple of them asked where I got their names. Naturally I couldn't tell them about the list that crazy Rachel filched for you."

"She just photocopied it," Congo said.

"Hillman may be a schemer," Lester said, "but so far you're the only one who has pulled anything illegal."

"That we know about," Congo corrected. "See if you can find out who owns this place"

"The Lodge?"

"The manager wants me to play poker. He's staking me."

"It's trouble, John."

"If I blow it off, they'll just blind-side me with something else. Better to keep them in front of me."

Congo hung up and returned to the conference room. The tables had been rearranged. Seating was by personality profile. The other controllers saw him coming.

"Here's Attila."

"We thought we'd lost you to pillage and plunder."

"I feel like the pillagee this trip," Congo said.

Hillman took the podium, smiling benevolently, to introduce the afternoon program. "Synergy," he lectured, "is the key to being competitive in the modern marketplace. The advantage once enjoyed by monarchs who brought together vast holdings by force of arms now accrues to groups of owners who can pool their resources and work in concert. Now let's all have some fun while we learn how to meld our individual strengths into an economic powerhouse."

Madison Palmer appeared to have appointed himself the leader of the four analyzers. He stood and cleared his throat.

"That's all very well, Royce, but we'd like some time to ask questions, to be sure we have all the facts."

The persuaders pounced on him.

"For God's sake, Madison, leave the dreary details to the lawyers."

"Poor old Madison is a lawyer."

"The bean counters, then."

An afternoon of exercises moderated by the facilitator engaged the different groups in emphasizing positive aspects of the Athens proposal. It was past five when Congo got back to his bungalow and called Los Angeles. He described the program to Abe Lester.

"They never once mentioned the details of the proposal."

"Sell the sizzle, not the steak," Lester quoted. "Anyone who lives on commission will tell you that."

"Did you find out who owns the Lodge?"

"Only Mexican citizens or corporations controlled by Mexican citizens can own real estate in Mexico. Anything beyond that, it's wire the pesos for a title search and we'll tell you manana."

Congo thanked Lester, showered and dressed in fresh slacks and shirt for dinner. His table assignment was at the rear of the room. Conversation established that the others at the table owned only minimal interests.

The poker game began a little past eight, in a spacious room off the lounge. A cocktail waitress circulated among the kibitzers. Congo was one of seven men playing. All but one represented ownership interests in the Elysian.

The outsider was Caris Pomeroy, who introduced himself as a stock broker. A man of mixed race and thirty some years, he dressed well in a casual way. His eyes had the steady sheen of contact lenses.

"Five card draw," he announced as he began dealing across the green baize of the table.

Players gathered up their cards as they arrived, arranging them into tight fans in their hands. Congo was the only exception. He made a pile of his, face down on the table, so that only the back of one showed.

"Why don't you pick them up?" Stuart Forrest asked.

Forty something, beefy and sleek, Forrest looked like old money. He represented, according to his alcoholic brother at Madison Palmer's, ninety one shares. Congo gave him a smile befitting his status.

"I'm a nervous player. The cards get sweaty if I handle them."

Betting began and Congo lifted his shot glass, turning it in his hand and looking through it as if considering the fluid inside. He put it down without drinking, took only one card. Betting escalated quickly and soon only Congo and Forrest remained in the game.

Forrest grinned wickedly. "You took one card, and you've been betting fifty a crack to bluff everybody into thinking you filled something. Well, I don't bluff. Here's your fifty, and another back."

That took the pot past a thousand dollars.

"Call." Congo matched the bet.

"Three bullets." Forrest put down three aces, showing each with a dramatic flourish.

Congo turned up five out-of-sequence cards, all diamonds. Low profanities went around the table.

"Goddamn flush."

"Tough luck, Stu."

Forrest eyed Congo closely. "How good are you?"

"I used to play for a living."

A small buzz arose.

Congo said, "I'll be glad to check out if anyone's nervous about that. Or I can pass my deal."

"No way," Forrest said with a grin. "I always wanted to know if I could face down a pro."

Congo declared five card stud for his deal, extending his prerogative to call odds on making various hands as he dealt the up cards. He dropped his own hand after betting thirty dollars without developing anything. One of the players believed Congo's odds and stayed with two tens against Forrest's strong bet that he could better a pair of sevens. Forrest was not happy about losing.

"Let's just call the possible hands. Leave the players to figure their own odds."

"Hell, Stu, give us a break."

"You don't have to win all the time."

"Yeah. Congo's going to cream us anyway. We might as well learn something."

The deal progressed around the table. Congo played conservatively, restricting his losses on poor hands, betting the good ones strictly according to mathematics, never bluffing. He drank sparingly from his shot glass, but held it often, peering into the liquid as if seeking guidance.

Others at the table drank freely. Off color jokes began to circulate. Congo tried a few one liners to ridicule Royce Hillman, the Athens proposal and the day's session. He got a few laughs, but no serious interest. Forrest tried without success to bait him into high bets. Pomeroy watched the two men closely for a few hands. On his next deal, he called for a new deck.

"Five card draw," he announced. "Time to get back to the real thing."

Betting opened and Congo took three cards.

Forrest stood pat.

"Up a hundred," Congo said when his bet came around.

Other players dropped quickly.

Forrest smiled. "Your hundred and fifty back."

"Your hand is a little like Athens," Congo said. "It looks good on the surface, but you'll regret backing it."

"See me, raise or fold."

"What I got from our nice dealer, were my third and fourth nine." Congo put fifty dollars on the table.

Forrest laughed. "If you're lying, you're a bad bluff artist. If you're not, you're the worst poker player I ever saw."

"My real game is canasta," Congo said.

Forrest was not amused. Judging from random remarks he had dropped during the evening, poker was sacred to him. Anyone who ridiculed it made light of his manhood. He set down a full house, aces over fours. Congo turned the four nines. More profanities went around the table.

"Hand like that, you should've raised him through the roof."

"Stu would've taken you to the cleaners if the cards were reversed."

Forrest glared. "I don't need charity."

Congo smiled and gathered his pot. "I'll leave now, gentlemen, and make room for someone with some skill."

One of the kibitzers replaced him immediately.

Congo's smile evaporated as soon as he was out of the room. He made directly for Segura's office, rapped on the door and went in unbidden. Segura was in the middle of a telephone call. Congo ignored a shake of the manager's head, walked to the desk and counted down his two thousand dollar stake. He stuffed a sizable remaining sheaf of bills into his pocket and sat down to wait for Segura to finish.

The manager cradled the telephone delicately. He considered Congo's angry eyes, spoke thoughtfully.

"That didn't take long."

"What was the plan?" Congo demanded. "Was Mr. Pomeroy, or whatever his real name is, supposed to rig the game so I humiliated Forrest?"

"I don't understand."

"It wouldn't take long for word to get around that I had been a professional gambler, nor long for word of what had happened to alienate the other owners of the Elysian."

"And why would I wish to do that?"

"Royce Hillman is either a silent owner or financier of this lodge. I doubt that he found it in a travel brochure."

Segura didn't move a muscle. His voice had the same innkeeper's accommodating blandness as his smile. "I asked only that you investigate cheating."

"Which you knew to be happening because you commissioned it. Your system needs work, by the way. The contact lenses are pretty obvious, and polarized light markings can be read through certain kinds of liquor glasses, held at the proper angle. Suits were marked in the corners and values in the wheel pattern on the backs. The nines were belly-stripped and the aces end-shaved so they could be stacked and dealt by touch."

A fleeting scowl touched Segura's features. "Mr. Pomeroy came highly recommended."

"There are private investigators who specialize in gaming fraud. They are good enough to catch any mechanic you can find. If a suspicious loser sends one in, and one day there will be a suspicious loser, it will cost the lodge a lot more than you ever pick up fleecing the fat cats."

"Thank you, Mr. Congo. I shall pass along your recommendation."

Segura's eyes were opaque, impossible to read.

Congo left.

He had played for less than an hour, and the night's activity was just beginning. The walls to the dining area had been removed to expand the lounge into a dance floor. Congo tapped a samba rhythm on the bar while he waited for a Cuba Libre but stopped when he saw Karen Steele among the dancers.

22

Karen was rhythmic and radiant in a sleeveless dress. Her dance partner was one of the Elysian owners. He had two left feet, no knowledge of Latin dance and enough liquor in him not to care. Congo nibbled his drink and made no effort to hide his displeasure.

When the number ended, Karen and her partner went laughing out to the patio where several large tables were set up. They sat at one occupied by several Elysian owners and their wives. Congo pasted a smile on his face and went out after them.

The last glow of the sun silhouetted the distant mountains that formed the spine of Baja California. Conversation drifted, punctuated by the occasional sizzle of a bug settling on one of the electric traps disguised as tropical torches. Congo moved a chair to the table where Karen and the Elysian owners sat.

"Hi folks," he said cheerfully. "Mind if I join you?"

"No, Hell, sit down," a well-oiled voice said.

"We're ordering escargot smothered in catsup," another chimed in.

"Red snails in the sunset," the table said in ragged unison, bringing a chorus of inebriated laughter.

"Thought you were in playing poker with Stu Forrest and the macho crowd," someone said.

"I made the mistake of suggesting we switch to canasta," Congo replied.

Another laugh went around the table. Karen wasn't in on the joke. She smiled when the others made room for Congo to sit across from her.

"I'm glad you could come, John."

"So am I," he said.

Her eyes offered no encouragement. "What did you think of the presentation?"

"I'm not sure what it had to do with Athens or the Elysian Hotel."

More laughter, followed by commentary:

"The view from the controller's group."

"The Hitler youth."

"Seig Heil."

Congo laughed along with the others. "At my age, I'll take youth any way it comes."

Karen smiled in confusion. The table pitched in with explanations:

"Royce's shrink divided us into personality groups."

"The controllers had the longest list of objections."

"Mostly objecting to the fact that they weren't running things."

"My way or the highway."

"If they had their way, they'd shut down the whole deal and put you out of a job."

Congo raised his eyebrows at Karen.

"I've accepted the position of Vice President for Leasing with Athens," she told him.

A round of applause from the table brought a flush to her cheeks. Congo blinked the surprise out of his expression.

"Congratulations," he said, and raised his glass in a toast. "Those of us who depended on your brokerage services will be devastated but I guess that's progress."

"Progress," several of the group repeated.

While they drank Madison Palmer arrived at the table and loomed beside Congo's chair.

"Have you seen Adrienne?"

"Not since I spoke to the two of you at dinner."

"I thought she might have been with you."

Congo shook his head. "I've been playing cards."

Palmer glanced at his friends around the table, as if looking for some hint that Congo might be lying. He got only nods of agreement. Worry etched lines into his forehead. He hurried off without quite seeming to know where he was going.

"Poor Madison," a man said when he was out of earshot. "Adrienne's just too much for him to handle."

The women had their own ideas:

"She's a free spirit."

"Something you men wouldn't understand."

"Mexico, the land of romance," another man said. "You've got to move fast here, even with your wife."

His own wife began teasing him, and the rest of the group joined in with gusto.

Congo winked at Karen. "Would you like to dance?"

"I'd love to."

She rose quickly, as if she didn't want to miss an opportunity to get him away from the others. They reached the dance floor as the small orchestra began an intimate rumba. Congo held her gently, as closely as she would allow, guiding her expertly through a swirl of dancers.

"Very few men can do an actual rumba," she marveled.

"I took a lot of lessons on a lot of cruise ships."

"Do you like to travel?" she asked.

"I was working. The dance lessons were cover."

"Working? Does that mean gambling?"

"If the cruise staff thought you were there to romance the widows, they didn't mind if you won a few dollars in their shiny new casino."

"Did you enjoy the widows?"

"I was a perfect gentleman."

She laughed, a quick note of musical mockery. "I'd better send this dress to Goodwill. It must make me look terribly gullible."

"I'm serious," he said. "When you work in a recreational industry, it's important not to get distracted by play."

"Oh, God, I don't believe this. I'm dancing in the tropic sunset while a suave gambler pours out his sins to me. Where were you when I was nineteen?"

"You're nineteen tonight."

She tensed when he tried to draw her closer. "Did you always win? On the cruise ships?"

He gave her a little room, accepted her change of subject. "Games of chance aren't about winning. They're about recognizing that over time you'll lose more often than you'll win and managing the process so you have more money when you step away from the table than you had when you sat down."

"Way more information than I needed," she chided, and then grew serious. "John, you don't have to hide behind the gambler's machismo and the good loser façade. If you're disappointed in me, just say so."

"I'm disappointed, sure," Congo admitted. "But I'm worried about you, too. I said what I did because I'm not sure you understand what Athens really involves."

The music ended and he took her hand and led her off the dance floor to a secluded corner.

"The mathematical principle is called regression to the mean," he explained. "In simple terms, no winning or losing streak lasts forever. If you watch the cards and know the odds, you can minimize your losses on the poor hands and win big when luck is on your side."

"I wonder if Gaylord Ravenal knew that," she said with a strained laugh.

"My apologies to Broadway, but real riverboat gamblers were cheats and compulsives who died broke."

"I was teasing," she said.

"One story goes that a riverboat gambler found one of his cronies in a game of three card monte on a wharf. He pulled him aside and said, 'What's the matter with you? That game is rigged.' The fellow answered, 'I know, but this is Sunday and it's the only game in town'."

Patience left her in an exasperated sigh. "John, I really think this conversation is—"

"Okay," he interrupted, holding his hands up in a placating gesture. "I'm not explaining this well but there is a point to it all, if you'll just hear me out."

She compressed her lips, said nothing.

"For Hillman," Congo pushed on, "Athens is the only game in town. His growth plans require a non-stop winning streak, which is a mathematical impossibility. The game is rigged against him, and anyone else who plays."

"Athens is a business deal," she said. "It's not some hit and run cruise boat scheme. It's permanent."

"The line between business and gambling is purely social," Congo said. "The mathematics and the risk management principles are exactly the same."

"You rolled the dice when you bought Crestline."

"For personal, not financial, reasons. Having a place to call home was more important to me than the next dollar I might make."

"Home is more than a place or a business," she said. "It's fitting in with the people around you. Being part of the community."

"The point is that I was ready to risk a large financial loss for personal reasons. Hillman may be doing the same with Athens. He may be risking it all to carve out a place in history."

"Royce is very conservative. His deals are carefully thought out and as safe as—"

The music had stopped and the silence amplified Karen's voice. Congo grinned at her sudden embarrassment and indicated the patio with his eyes, offering escape from prying ears.

"Look," he said as they skirted the dance floor, "the conversation has wandered from what I intended, but I do care about you. I don't want to see you hurt."

"It's sweet of you to worry, but I'm a big girl now. I have to take risks if I want to get ahead in life. I've never been afraid of challenges. My first sale was a nightmare called the Palladium. It used to be a ballroom. You should have seen it."

"The place in Hollywood?" he asked.

"Before they tore it down. Did you know it?"

"Small world," he said. "I went there once when I was young because T-Bone Walker was playing. Years later it was one of the stops I made to see if I really wanted to make a life in L.A. Standing there with the dust and the peeling paint and the smell of rodents dead behind the walls, I could still hear the guitar riffs of *Stormy Monday*."

"I'd better get back to the table," she said. "I'm the official hostess."

"And tomorrow?"

"I'm in charge of the horseback tour group." She laughed grimly. "It's been ten years since I've even seen a real horse. What about you?"

"I neglected to give Hillman's receptionist a preferred recreation when I called for my reservation, so it looks like I'll be hiking up some canyon hunting javelina."

"What's javelina?"

"Some kind of wild pig. Why anybody would want to shoot one, I have no idea."

"If you're really concerned about the Athens proposal," she said on the way across the patio, "maybe I can set up a private meeting with Royce."

"I've talked Hillman's ear off."

A wolf-whistle came from the table.

"Enough romance, you two."

"Back to the party."

Congo whispered his bungalow number in Karen's ear. "I'm going to get some rest. It's going to be a hundred ten degrees again tomorrow. Come by if you want to talk."

She smiled, shook her head and returned to the table. Congo left the patio and followed a meandering stone path.

Away from the buzz of conversation the evening was peaceful. Crickets added their refrain to the dance music. An unseen tropical bird made its presence known. Passing his bungalow, he went down to the sea wall to gaze out over the Gulf of California.

The gentle lap of waves on the endless white sand wasn't quite enough to cover the quiet footsteps approaching from behind.

23

Adrienne Palmer materialized out of the tropical evening. Moonlight drew a sharp contrast between sun-bronzed skin and the white of a halter and shorts. An unsteady sway brought her along the path to the sea wall where Congo stood. She stopped just short of colliding with him and stood on her toes to bring her face within inches of his.

"Tell me, good sir, is this beach topless, do you happen to know?"

Her tinkling laugh was full of mischief. She took two more wobbly steps to peer down over the sea wall and along the white beach.

"Because I don't see any signs that say it isn't," she said.

Congo made no move to steady her uncertain balance. "I'll leave my shirt on until I find out for sure."

She slurred, "Hole thish," and thrust a highball glass at him. When he didn't take it, she let it fall, laughing when it shattered on the stone path. She fumbled with the front clasp of her halter.

Congo said, "Good night, Mrs. Palmer," and started along the path that led to his bungalow.

She caught up with him and took his arm. Her halter was unfastened. Breasts threatened to bounce themselves free of loose hanging fabric. Congo limited himself to eye contact.

"Your husband was looking for you earlier."

"Oh, pooh. I can do Madison any time."

"The two of you can work that out," Congo said. "I'm going to bed."

"Do you suggest bed to all the stray women you find on lonely beaches? Or just the ones trying to liberate their hooters?"

"What's this about?" Congo asked.

"You broke my glass. That means I get to raid your liquor cabinet."

"Your lush act is no better than it was in Pacific Palisades," he said. "And the wayward wife routine is getting worse by the minute."

"Now why ever would a swinging bachelor object to a wayward wife?"

"Is there any chance for an intelligent conversation here?"

Her voice dropped all pretense of intoxication. "I did ask you politely to leave Madison alone."

"I have."

She gave his arm an impatient tug. "I know about the lawsuit you two plan to file."

Congo stopped short and stared at her. "What lawsuit?"

"The one to stop the Athens project," she said and put a chastising fingertip to the end of his nose when he scowled.

Congo resumed his walk, morose and lost in thought. She caught up with him and took his arm again.

"Poor, dear Madison gets so caught up in his childish crusades."

"I don't know about any lawsuit, but poor, dear Madison is on the right track. The next slump in office rents could take Hillman's bright idea straight into bankruptcy."

"Do you know how long Royce has been in real estate?"

"Probably about as long as Richard Nixon was in politics before Watergate." They reached Congo's bungalow and he tried to disengage his arm.

"Open up," she insisted. "Unless you want me to let out a piercing scream."

Mambo rhythm drifted on the warm, perfumed air. They were within earshot of the lounge. Congo unlocked the door, stepped quickly through and flipped on the lights.

An empty room mocked his precautions.

Adrienne went to the window and flung open the draperies. "Have you ever wanted to say hello to Buffalo with no clothes on?"

"No." Congo picked up the telephone.

"Who are you calling?"

"Housekeeping. I want the place cleaned out."

"Tomorrow." She used a manicured finger to disconnect the call. "You're being a very bad host. You haven't asked me what I want to drink."

"Give it a rest, Mrs. Palmer."

Congo reestablished the call. A woman's voice came over the line, asking in Latin-inflected English how she could help.

"Pedro Segura, please," Congo said. "Use the radio to find him if you have to."

Adrienne Palmer strutted back and forth in front of the window, slowly running the zipper at the side of her shorts.

"I always have wanted to say hello to Buffalo with no clothes on, and I'm damn well going to do it."

The phone came alive. "This is Pedro Segura. How can I help you?"

"John Congo, Mr. Segura. Find Madison Palmer. Tell him to come down to my bungalow and get his wife the hell out of here."

"Is there a problem, Mr. Congo?"

"Not if you don't mind your resort looking like a Tijuana cat house."

"I will find Mr. Palmer."

Adrienne dropped her shorts.

"Tell him to bring a bath robe," Congo added.

Adrienne strutted over from the window in a white bikini bottom. "I bet you thought I really was going to go naked, didn't you?"

Congo hung up. "Tell me about this lawsuit your husband is filing."

She wagged a finger in his face. "Naughty, naughty. Mustn't try to fool Adrienne. She doesn't like it."

"Poor, dear Madison is on his way to collect you. We'll talk it over when he gets here."

She slapped his cheek with a light caress and strutted to the small refrigerator that held the bungalow's supply of refreshments.

"Yours was rum and coke, wasn't it?"

"The rum was your idea."

"Madison and I do talk, you know. He told me about the lawsuit. 'That Congo fellow knew a lot more than he let on the night he was out here. A lot more.' Madison's exact words."

Congo sat down. "The fact that I don't blab everything I know doesn't make me party to legal action."

Adrienne brought him his drink. "If Madison is on his way, it must be time."

She shrugged out of her halter and slipped off the bikini bottom. Congo made a point of not staring.

"Are you a camera buff, John?" She laughed suddenly and musically. "Buff. Now there's a double meaning."

"I'm allergic to photographs," Congo said.

"Madison likes to shoot me in the nude. His own wife. Now that's a little warped, wouldn't you say?"

"I'd say it's none of my business."

She sat on the arm of his chair and reached for the top button of his shirt. He pushed her hand away. She pouted.

"I promise not to bite. Madison absolutely hates it when I—"

The door burst open, hit the wall stop and ricocheted to collide with Madison Palmer on his way in. He pushed it aside. Lordly calm had deserted him. He rushed to his wife and pulled her away from Congo.

"My God, Adrienne! Are you drunk?"

She smiled archly at Congo. "Now you see what you've gone and done, John. Getting me tipsy and seducing me has upset poor Madison."

Palmer glared at Congo. "I invited you into my home. And now I find you here with my wife."

"Sit down, Mr. Palmer. We need to talk."

"For God's sake, Adrienne, put on some clothes."

She waved at Congo and pranced around the room collecting her discarded apparel. Palmer stood looming over Congo. His nostrils moved in and out with harsh breathing.

"Normally I'd take you apart bone by bone, but this is bigger than just me."

"You two can work out your domestic issues later," Congo said. "Right now we need to talk business. Close the door and sit down."

"You think you've put one over, but I'm going to cut you down to size in court."

"Forget this silly soap opera," Congo ordered. "Sit down and tell me what you're nattering about."

Pedro Segura and Royce Hillman appeared at the open door. Segura came in quickly, moving to a position where he could intervene if things got physical.

"Mr. Palmer, please, I think things may not be just as they seem."

"You're right about that," Palmer said grimly.

Hillman patted Palmer's shoulder. "Take it easy, Madison. This will only make things worse."

Palmer pulled away, put an arm around Adrienne's shoulders and moved her toward the door.

She smiled back at Congo. "Oh, John, if I do turn out to be pregnant, promise me you won't start some awful custody battle. We don't want to humiliate poor Madison. At least not publicly."

Palmer hurried her out.

Segura closed the door. "Mr. Congo, I don't know exactly what took place, but—"

"Ask Hillman."

The executive smiled triumphantly. "Thank you, Mr. Segura. I don't think we need take any more of your time."

Segura smiled uncomfortably. "As you wish, Mr. Hillman."

He padded out and closed the door softly behind him, as if the quiet of his departure might ensure peace between the two men he was leaving behind.

Hillman guffawed. "Looks like you really stepped into it this time."

"And here I thought I was starring in Hillman players' production of *High Society Hi-Jinks*. Script by Doctor Ruth. Costumes by Victoria's Secret. Set decorations courtesy of Mexican rent-a-front. The preceding melodrama has been video-taped for release to our fighting shysters at the negotiating table."

Angry blood suffused Hillman's face. "My advice is to get your ass back to L.A., keep your mouth shut when you get there and vote your shares with the majority."

The executive turned and strode out.

Congo opened the jalousie windows to let in some fresh air. He called Los Angeles and described the evening to Abe Lester, starting with the poker game and then moving on to the news that Karen Steele had been tapped as an Athens executive.

"I told you so," Lester said. "I mean I don't like to say I told you so, but I fucking told you so. That broad is way out of your class. You should have known she was up to something."

Congo ignored the remark and launched into his encounter with Adrienne Palmer. "I haven't a clue what this lawsuit is about. Have we been served with anything?"

"I haven't seen shit. But you're liable to if this Palmer found his old lady in your bungalow in her birthday suit."

"That's another thing. The whole business was brainless and pointless. It wouldn't have made the cut for afternoon television."

"John, you're mostly scar tissue. Emotion doesn't have much impact on you. Other people aren't like that. If you get a reputation for playing with wives, you won't be leading any opposition to anything."

Congo made a face. "Palmer isn't likely to advertise. I can catch up with him tomorrow and talk some sense into him. We're both scheduled for the hunting trip."

"How smart is that?" Lester asked.

"What do you suggest?"

"A little common sense?" Lester said without much optimism. "I mean, you've got Hillman and Forrest and Palmer and God knows who else pissed at you, and tomorrow you're all going off into the badlands with loaded rifles."

24

The next morning's breakfast conversation buzzed with the mixture of anticipation and dread that preceded unfamiliar activities. Karen Steele was formally introduced as Athens' Vice President for Leasing and an African-American gentleman was named Chief Financial Officer. Hillman, Easter and the two new officers each would lead one of the day's four recreational groups.

Congo and eight other men were loaded into open Jeeps. Asphalt paving took them as far as the airfield. Beyond that a dirt track curved up a broad-floored canyon. Several young Mexican men in wide-brimmed hats and informal Lodge livery waited at a shooting range set against a hillside. The hunters dismounted in the shade of a small grove. Pat Easter addressed the group.

"Gentlemen, before we try our luck, our guides will give us a few pointers on marksmanship. Let's take this opportunity to break out of our comfort zones and get to know each other."

The guides issued ear valves and .25/20 rifles with numbers stenciled on the stocks. Congo received the low number. He was assigned to shoot first, a group of three rounds. Stuart Forrest volunteered to shoot with him.

They sat at either end of a bench at a picnic table. Sandbags were set on the table to make rifle rests. Two bulls-eye targets squatted in the scrub brush down range. Forrest peered through the micrometer sights of the custom-made .222 he had brought with him.

"Five hundred on the first group?" he suggested.

"I'm trying to save money," Congo said. "I'll need it if the Athens deal goes through."

"You sure you're not just yellow?"

"I'm sure I am. I make a point of it."

Concentration creased Forrest's meaty good looks as he fired. Congo shot deliberately. When the targets were retrieved, Forrest's three shots lay in a one inch cluster. Two of Congo's three holes were within a millimeter of touching. The other was less than half an inch away.

"That's luck," Forrest grumbled. "The damned rifle isn't that accurate."

Congo was happy to agree.

A few spectators laughed.

"Give it up, Stu."

"You'll never beat him."

"He's got your number."

Forrest and Congo surrendered their rifles to a guide. They stepped back into the group to make room for the next two shooters. Forrest shoved his target into a trash barrel.

"What's your hunting experience?"

"I do well to find what I want in a supermarket."

"You didn't learn to shoot like that in the produce aisle."

"I grew up in a carnival."

Forrest laughed. "You're still shooting at tin ducks. Why don't you get on the right side of the Athens deal?"

"For the same reason I wouldn't try to fill an inside straight unless the pot was at least twelve times the bet."

Mention of poker left Forrest sulking.

After everyone had shot the party was briefed. They would hunt in three man groups, each with its own guide. Congo positioned himself close to Madison Palmer.

Easter had a list prepared.

Congo wound up with Stuart Forrest and Paul Clive, the bird-nosed attorney Congo had met at Palmer's. Clive had spent time in an upscale outdoor outfitter.

"What about snakes?" he asked, glancing down at his new boots as if he had been warned he would need the protection they afforded.

"Snakes are usually quiet during the heat of the day," the guide said. "They will not strike unless you get too close or provoke them. Simply give them plenty of room. They will show you the same courtesy."

Wide brimmed straw hats and canteens were handed out. Cleaned rifles were re-issued. Guides supervised loading and securing. The groups separated and positioned themselves in a line stretching the width of the canyon.

A call came over a radio in the guide's shirt pocket. He replied in Spanish, addressed his group in English.

"We will begin in five minutes. Stay abreast and keep five paces between you. Watch for any sign of chewed cactus. The wind is blowing down the canyon toward us, so the pig will not smell us coming. His eyes are bad and his hearing is not so good either. If we move carefully, we can get within fifty yards. Only the designated shooter will take his rifle off safety, and only with my permission. Who will take the first shot?"

Congo slung his rifle.

Forrest scowled. "What's the matter? Not so sure of yourself with a moving target?"

"I'm not interested in shooting animals."

"Why did you sign up if you don't like hunting?"

"I neglected to sign up for anything. Apparently the other groups were full."

Clive fidgeted and glanced at Congo. "What if one of these things charges us? You're the best shot here."

The guide tried to keep amusement out of his smile. "Javelina is not European boar, sir. Please do not worry for your safety."

Forrest gave Clive a sharp glance. "I'll take the first shot. You can get a look at a dead one before you have to face his brothers."

The guide placed Congo at the left of the group with an admonition to stay in sight and abreast of the group on his left. "Do not move too quickly, gentlemen. If we get ahead, we could find ourselves in the field of fire of another group."

They made their way up the canyon under a relentless sun. The guide politely enforced water and salt discipline. The morning wore on. A rifle shot echoed across the canyon from the left. Another followed in quick succession. The guide halted them and listened briefly to his radio.

"The first kill has been made," he said with an encouraging smile.

Forrest seemed disappointed. "Well, maybe ours will be bigger."

A Jeep brought box lunches and took down the carcass. The three groups ate together in the shade of a rock outcrop. Madison Palmer sat a little apart from the others, where he could remove his boots. Congo went over and sat beside him.

"I'm not having any fun either," he said, and opened his lunch box to find what was probably intended as a Caesar salad.

Palmer ignored Congo to explore tender spots on his feet. Weight sagged at his midsection and wisps of his usually perfect hair straggled out from under his straw hat.

"Your wife mentioned that you were planning to file suit to stop the Athens project," Congo persisted.

"Leave Adrienne out of this."

"She seemed to think you and I were filing together."

"Adrienne has no legal training." Palmer grimaced as he pushed one foot into a boot. "Sometimes she misconstrues."

"What is the basis of the suit?"

"I think you know." Palmer got his other boot on, stood and limped off to eat with Paul Clive.

After the meal the hunters resumed their climb into the canyon. The ground grew steeper and rougher. The afternoon sun was withering, shade nonexistent. The first break found Congo breathing raggedly, his shirt soaked in sweat.

"How far have we come?" he asked as the guide watched him wash down the mandatory salt tablet.

"About three kilometers, sir."

Clive looked back down the canyon at the endless blue of the Gulf of California. "How many vertical feet?"

"Perhaps a thousand, sir."

Forrest was as adamant as he was drained. "We came for pig. We stay at it until we score. Nobody wimps out."

Clive looked at the guide. "Are we doing that badly?"

"No, sir. Very few hunts make it this far. There is only another kilometer or so where there is vegetation for the pigs to feed. But it is prime ground because it has not been hunted."

Forrest stood. "Well let's go, then."

"As soon as the other groups are ready, sir."

They set off in another five minutes, moving cautiously into worsening terrain. The guide stopped them.

"Javelina," he said very quietly, pointing at an irregularly chewed cactus leaf.

"Where?" Forrest whispered, peering up the canyon as he slipped his rifle off safety.

"Not yet, sir." The guide reached over and put the safety back on. "Look for tracks."

They moved slowly forward, scanning the ground. Congo kept an eye to his left. The adjacent group was beginning to pull ahead.

"There," the guide said softly.

"Where?" Forrest peered intently.

"Look at one o-clock, about seventy meters," the guide said. "Where the cactus appears broken."

Forrest threw his rifle to his shoulder and fired. A small puff of dust rose from the cactus. A squeal of pain was followed by the erratic scurrying of a small, wounded animal, half seen. The guide had already shouldered his rifle. He fired immediately. Another puff of dust, then stillness. The guide fished the radio from his pocket.

"I will have your trophy picked up, Mr. Forrest."

The guide's call stopped the other groups. He made sure all rifles were secured, and then they trudged up to inspect the carcass, lying deflated in a thicket of cactus.

Dark blood matted the bristles where Forrest's bullet had torn through the creature's lungs. More dribbled from its snout. A repulsive smell rose. Paul Clive paled and stepped back.

Congo caught him before he could stumble. "That's victory, Mr. Clive. Up close and personal."

Forrest said, "Take a salt tablet, Paul. The next shot is yours."

Congo said, "You don't have to, Clive. We can chalk up the rest of the afternoon to exercise."

A sharp glance from Forrest said otherwise.

The group set off as soon as the jeep recovered the carcass. Arduous minutes dragged into half an hour. A rifle shot echoed across the canyon. The guide called a halt.

Congo sat sweating on a rock and watched the Jeep hurry up the canyon toward the group on his left. There seemed to be considerable excitement, but they were too far for voices to carry clearly. The guide's radio emitted a crackle of Spanish.

He replied briefly, and then addressed the group. "Gentlemen, I am afraid we must return."

"Why?" Forrest demanded.

"There has been an accident."

Forrest and Clive scrambled to where Congo sat. The Jeep reached the group on their left. A man was lifted and placed in back. Clive squinted against the afternoon sun.

"Who is it?"

Forrest took a pair of compact binoculars from his shirt pocket and trained them on the Jeep.

"Madison Palmer."

Congo tensed, looked at the guide. "What happened?"

"We must wait here. A Jeep will come for us."

The wait was sweltering, the ride down rough and dirty. Grit pasted itself to sweat soaked faces. Activity was visible around the airfield at the base of the canyon. Blue strobe lights marked the rapid progress of a police vehicle along the access road. A medical airlift helicopter blew billowing clouds of dust as it touched down.

"Looks serious," Forrest said.

"Madison has been grumbling about this hunt ever since Adrienne signed him up for it," Clive said. "If that's a broken leg, it'll really put the icing on things."

Forrest smiled, his teeth a white mockery in the grime of his face. "What do you think, Congo? You know Adrienne Palmer, don't you?"

"I've met her."

"I meant know in the Biblical sense." Triumph boomed in Forrest's laugh, notice to the world that he had put one over on his nemesis.

The helicopter lifted off as the Jeep reached the airfield, blowing a final, filthy insult over the passengers. They climbed down coughing dust from their throats.

Peter Segura brought over a police official. "Mr. Congo, may I present Sub-Teniente Morales."

The police sub-lieutenant was a short, rotund man who took great care with his grooming. The knife edge creases of his brown uniform bent over his stomach like the stitching on a soccer ball. Heavy jowls accented the gravity of his expression.

"Mr. Congo," he said with a thick Latin accent, "I understand you argued with the man who was shot."

25

Dust from the departed helicopter settled like fallout from a mushroom cloud, mottling the spit-shine of Morales' shoes and the reflective brim of his uniform cap, making specks on the grayish lenses of his light sensitive spectacles. The police official held out a plump hand.

"Mr. Congo, I will inspect your rifle."

A motorcycle officer stood a few feet away. He moved his hand to the butt of a holstered automatic.

Congo unslung the rifle from his shoulder and surrendered the weapon, careful to keep his hand away from the trigger. Morales opened the action. A cartridge popped out into his fingers. He sniffed at the aroma of solvent still present in the chamber.

"This has not been fired since it was last cleaned."

"No." Congo had to cough dust from his throat.

"Were you not hunting, sir?"

"I just went along for the hike."

Morales' questioning glance at the group produced only confirming nods. The Sub-Lieutenant handed Congo's rifle to the officer and gave instructions in Spanish. The guide informed Forrest and Clive that all rifles would be confiscated. Morales took out a white handkerchief and wiped his fingers clean of any residue of manual labor.

"Mr. Congo, you will accompany me, please."

Morales led the way into the hangar, moving his short legs in a smart, military stride. He appropriated an office, shooing the occupant out with a few curt words. Once he had seated himself behind the desk, his manner was less abrupt. He removed his cap, blew bits of dust from the brim and set it on the desk. After he had performed the same ritual with his spectacles, he waved Congo to a facing chair. His voice was as bland as his expression.

"I am told there was an incident involving you and the injured man's wife in your bungalow last night."

It wasn't so much a question as an opportunity for Congo to blurt something in his defense. Congo remained silent.

"I am eager to have your perspective on the matter," Morales said. "Please be complete and detailed."

He smiled patiently; a man who had all the time in the world to listen. Congo opened his canteen and rinsed his throat.

"I'm not sure where you want me to start."

"Did you know Mr. Palmer in the United States?"

"I met him. Once."

"And his wife?"

"I met her at the same time."

"Is that when you began seeing her?"

"There was no relationship," Congo said.

"My information is that Mr. Palmer found his wife in your bungalow under compromising circumstances. That is putting it delicately."

"That's not quite the whole story," Congo said. "I called Segura and asked him to find Palmer and send him to remove his wife from my bungalow."

The little room was an oven. Perspiration made streaks down the filth on Congo's face. Morales didn't seem to notice the temperature.

"Do you know who shot Mr. Palmer?"

"I didn't know anyone had been shot. The guide said only that there had been an accident."

"And you say you were only along for the hike."

"You've verified that I didn't fire my rifle."

"It is the hiking that confuses me," Morales said. "The American tourists who come here to hike, and there are many, have a certain look to them. They do not seem to think they can walk unless they wear expensive shoes and colorful sweatbands and carry fanny packs full of nutrition bars."

Congo took out a handkerchief and wiped sweat from his eyes.

"Of course, one might speculate," Morales went on, interlacing manicured fingers over his ample midsection and gazing up at a slow-turning ceiling fan, "that the hike wasn't part of the original plan. That something occurred during your stay to make you change your mind." He lowered his gaze to Congo. "Perhaps," he continued significantly, "you learned that you might have the satisfaction of seeing a romantic rival fall."

Congo shook his head, the irritability of fatigue visible in his movement.

"You must have had some reason to undertake so arduous an activity," Morales persisted.

"If I'd known what to expect, I'd have spent the day on the beach."

Morales smiled without amusement. "Thank you, Mr. Congo. I regret that we will need a formal statement before we can release your passport and allow you return to the United States. This we cannot do until tomorrow. Hopefully no information will surface that will compel us to detain you longer."

Congo stood. "Is Palmer going to be all right?"

"I am sure he will receive the best of care."

The hangar was bustling and no one challenged Congo when he left. He trudged back to his bungalow along the coast road, locking himself in when he arrived.

Peeling off his soiled clothes, he stepped into the shower. Water ran dirty for several minutes before it rinsed his hair clean and flushed out his pores. He dressed, sank into a chair and lifted the telephone. There was a soft tap at the door before he could place his call. He padded warily across the carpet and opened the door to the limit of the chain.

Karen Steele met his precautions with a questioning smile. "Is this a bad time?"

"No." Congo unchained the door and let her in.

She removed a wide-brimmed sun hat and shook her hair free. She smelled lightly of fragrant soap. Her outfit of Bermuda shorts and a sleeveless blouse had been selected with the knowledge that suggestion was more intriguing than display. Congo shot a surreptitious glance outside before he closed the door.

Karen had settled into a chair when he turned back. "I can't believe how much a simple ride took out of me. I know I'm going to feel it tomorrow. I don't even want to think about where."

"That's one advantage of the hunting trip. Only my feet will be sore."

"I heard what happened." Her voice fell to an uneasy whisper. "Were you there when …?"

Congo sat in a chair facing her. "Palmer and I were in different groups."

Her smile lost its habitual buoyancy. "Well, I suppose if you want to hunt, there are risks."

"The safety procedures were air-tight and closely supervised."

They stared at each other through a minute of silence. She brought her eyelids halfway down and considered him through the lashes.

"Several of the women warned me about you."

An inquisitive frown creased Congo's brow.

"On the ride today," she went on. "They said Madison Palmer caught his wife in your bungalow last night."

An idea flickered in the depths of Congo's eyes and with it came brooding silence.

"You don't like to talk," she observed.

"I thought I'd already bored you to tears with my life story."

"I don't mean your past or your aspirations. Things you've had time to develop pat explanations for. I mean things that are happening now. Spontaneous things. Things you haven't thought through yet."

Congo conceded the point with a shrug. "How did the retreat work out for you and Hillman?"

"The final nose count is 52% of the shares in favor of the Athens proposal, 19% against and 29% undecided or unknown. Royce is bound to pick up some of the undecideds, even if a few supporters have second thoughts."

"Have you signed a formal employment contract?"

Her smile was tentative. "I hope there are no hard feelings."

"I'd probably have done the same."

"I'm not sure that isn't just the gambler who has learned to lose gracefully."

"Does it really matter to you?"

"You'll be one of the owners of Athens. I'll be a new officer."

"Strictly business, then?"

"I would like to be friends."

"So would I," he confessed.

She stood and put on her hat. "Are you flying back tonight?"

He rose to open the door. "I'll have to stay over for the police inquiry."

She wished him luck and left. Congo phoned Abe Lester in Los Angeles and filled him in.

"Jesus Fucking Christ, John, this whole trip has been a fiasco. I mean, this Hillman character has been in the driver's seat the whole way."

"Then why have Palmer shot?" Congo asked.

"You think Hillman was behind that?"

"I know he tried to discredit me," Congo said. "What I don't understand is why. Karen said he had at least 52% of the vote locked up. More than enough to win."

"Christ, John, are you still talking to that broad?"

"She just stopped by for a minute."

"Cooling the mark," Lester said sourly. "Nothing like a little sympathy from a class chick to keep the suckers from screaming."

"Back off," Congo snapped. "I know how the long con works."

"Well, at least now you know where you stand."

"The problem," Congo said, "is that I don't. Hillman's moves make no sense. When you've got the game won, you throw the losers a consolation prize and split with the swag. You don't risk it all by having someone shot. I need to talk to Palmer to find out what he knows that made him a target."

"Oh, yeah, like he'll want to talk to you. I mean suppose he takes it into his head to tell the Mexican cops it was you who popped him? Just to get even because he thinks you're banging his old lady?"

"Les, you're a ray of sunshine in a world of gloom."

"Well, Christ, John, the Mexican cops are going to find out about your trouble in L.A. They'll probably hear about that loser you popped in Portland. None of it's going to look good."

"What to you want me to do? Go back and re-live my life?"

Lester relented with a drawn out sign. "We're burying Phil day after tomorrow. Any chance you can make it?"

"I don't know, Les. Right now I have no answers, no passport, no nothing."

26

Next morning the nine guests in the hunting party were taken by Jeep to the nearby town. The Mexicans who served Playa Blanca's visiting elite lived in close-packed adobe houses. Big-eyed children stared at the passing caravan and ran after it in a swirling wake of dust.

The police station was a low stucco building notable for worn linoleum floors and hard wooden furniture. Statements took most of the morning. Subteniente Morales, looking crisp in a fresh uniform, remained in his office.

The guests were driven back to the lodge and fed a sequestered lunch. Passports were released immediately afterward. Congo and Forrest were the only two with private planes at their disposal. A Jeep took them to the airfield. Forrest was somber.

"I guess poor Madison didn't make it."

"No?" Congo's eyes narrowed.

"I savvy more Espanol than I let on. I overheard Segura talking to that Sub-Teniente what's-his-name about arrangements to ship the body back to L.A."

"Did you happen to hear how he was shot?" Congo asked.

"Segura's pushing the accident theory. Every shot from the lodge group was accounted for, so there must have been someone else hunting in the canyon."

"Is that why we're being run out of the country?" Congo asked.

Forrest let out a grim laugh. "So you got that feeling, too?"

"Yesterday Palmer was alive and the police were looking for answers. Today he's dead and it's 'here's your hat, what's your hurry?'"

"Well, you can't blame them. The owners have mucho dinero at risk and the town depends on the lodge for its livelihood. The wrong publicity could cost everyone."

"What do you think happened?" Congo asked.

"You had a better view than I did," Forrest reminded him. "Hell, I'm still wondering where those four nines came from."

"The Easter Bunny brought them."

"If the dealer was cheating, why didn't you call him on it?"

"What's the point?" Congo asked. "There will always be someone nicking the suckers. Pomeroy's chair wouldn't have had time to get cold."

The Jeep stopped at the converted Air Force T-37 jet trainer Forrest flew for recreation. The driver got out to unload his luggage. Forrest opened his door but paused.

"Look, Congo, I'm going to be the Elysian's representative on the Athens board. I'll have more influence if I have all the major Elysian owners behind me. And I don't forget who my friends are."

"I'll keep that in mind."

They shook hands and Forrest got out.

Congo said, "Sucker," under his breath.

The driver ferried him down the flight line to his shiny old Duchess. "I have heard many wonderful things about Los Angeles," the youth said as he transferred Congo's bags.

"City of the dead," Congo said, handing over a few pesos. "People go there to be buried."

◆   ◆   ◆

"Were your ambitions worth Clint's life?"

Eileen Phillips sat erect on the rear seat of the limousine, staring straight ahead. Her veiled profile was briefly stark in the flashing motorcycle strobes that had stopped morning traffic so the funeral procession could turn into the cemetery. Congo's nostrils twitched at the perfume that suffused the tonneau.

"Phil was shot by a confused woman lashing out at a world she didn't understand."

"He was helping you evict her."

"It's part of the business, Eileen. Once in a great while it goes terribly wrong. I'm sorry Phil had to be in the way when it did."

The limousine drew up the curving cemetery drive and eased to a stop. Congo got out and held the door. Eileen made no effort to keep her tight black skirt from riding up long model's legs as she got out. In three-inch heels she stood as tall as Congo.

"You never gave a damn about Clint." She sniffled. "All you cared about was your Horatio Alger act. Orphan from the carnival makes good. Just don't ask how many people he stepped on to do it."

"All right, Eileen. Enough is enough. We still have a chance to bury him with a little dignity."

"We shouldn't quarrel."

She took his arm and pressed close as they waited to follow the casket. At graveside he installed her in a chair and stepped back to stand behind her.

Cars drew up behind the limousine and a somber crowd gathered. Some did business with Crestline. Others were young; probably friends Phillips had made playing amateur sports. The minister had the burly, agile look of a former athlete.

"As Clinton Jeffrey Phillips passes into the care of the Lord," he began, "let us cherish the memory of a selfless spirit. There was no better team player, on or off the field. But when his own crises came he faced them alone rather than impose on his friends."

Eileen reached up and took Congo's hand. She brought it close to her face.

"Clinton Jeffrey Phillips was not an important man in the sense of wealth or power or fame," the minister continued. "His importance lay in humility and common strength, in his willingness to follow those who sought to lead when they were right, in the courage he found to challenge them when they were wrong, in his commitment to strive daily for the wisdom to know the difference."

Eileen nestled Congo's hand in the curve of her neck, barely maintaining the façade of a grieving ex-spouse clinging for comfort as the minister droned on.

"For Clinton Jeffrey Phillips we return ashes unto ashes, dust unto dust, in the sure and certain hope of resurrection. For ourselves, let us think ahead to the day when we will meet him again and he will ask us what we have done in the time apart. Let us strive to conduct our lives so we may answer proudly when that day comes."

When the service was over, Congo installed a disappointed Eileen in the limousine and sent her off alone. He rode back in Abe Lester's Toyota.

"How the hell did she get herself appointed administrator of Phil's estate?" Congo asked.

"He never got around to changing his will after the divorce," Lester said. "Who expects to die when they're twenty-nine?"

"Women," Congo said sourly. He took out his cell phone and pressed a number. "Could I speak to Adrienne Palmer please? ... Yes, I understand this is a difficult time. Please give her this message. John Congo needs to meet with her. At her convenience but as soon as possible."

Congo left his office, home and cell phone numbers.

Lester broke the following silence uncertainly. "What about that guy Palmer? This morning's paper called it a hunting accident."

"A homicide investigation wouldn't be good for business at the lodge. And it could focus embarrassing publicity on the Athens deal."

"You think he was killed?"

"Did the police who talked to you and Phil after Raymond was killed say they were homicide detectives?" Congo asked.

"They wanted to know if you had Raymond killed."

"Hit," Congo corrected. "You said they said hit."

"What's the difference?"

"You and Phil both thought it was an odd word for them to use."

Lester shrugged. "Well, cops, you know. You expect them to use legal sounding language."

"They knew from the autopsy that Raymond had been punched in the stomach."

"You mean the cops just wanted to know if you told Phil to slug him?"

"Criminal intent," Congo said. "That's all they were after. If I told Phil to hit Raymond, that's assault and racketeering. If Phil hit him on a defensive impulse, that's no foul."

"What's that got to do with this Palmer?" Lester asked.

"My guess is there was no homicide investigation into Raymond's death because Hillman's lawyers convinced the police that it was an accident. Same-same Palmer in Mexico."

"Two down," Lester said with a glance at Congo. "One to go."

They finished the drive without speaking. Lester pulled into the drop-off zone in front of Crestline's office building.

"I need to pick up those retail audits," he said.

"Take the rest of the day off," Congo said. "You've earned it."

"And do what? I'm a numbers guy, John. That's where I go to hide."

Muffie sat behind the reception counter, activating the PBX. She hadn't changed from the somber business suit she had worn to the funeral. Her eyes wouldn't meet his.

"Is something wrong?" Congo asked.

She bit her lip, spoke nervously. "Do you remember I told you I once had a date with an FBI agent?"

"You told me you didn't like him."

"He called me when you were in Mexico. I was trying to think of a polite way to blow him off when he started in on this rant about how my life might be in danger and could I get out of the office and come to the Federal Building right away."

Congo's eyes narrowed. "Was your life in danger?"

She squirmed. "It sounds stupid to talk about now, but it was like totally real then."

"So you went?"

"There were like three people waiting for me in this conference room. There was Enrico. He's the Agent. He still creeps me out. And this Mr. Cravens. I've seen him on TV news. He's the head of the FBI office in L.A. And this freakish tall babe from the U.S. Attorney's office."

"What did they have to say?"

"That Mr. Cravens started going off about how you and Mr. Phillips and Mr. Lester were in organized crime. I was thinking this is so not true, but these people were way important and I didn't want to get in trouble arguing with them."

"What did they want?" Congo asked.

"They asked stuff like what I knew about Crestline and how you bought the company." Her voice fell to a fearful whisper. "They want me to copy any computer files you have on the bankruptcy."

Congo nodded. "They're all in the acquisition folder on the server. There's a CD burner built into my desktop. You'd better sign in under your logon ID, so the header record will look right to their technicians."

Her eyes rebelled at the idea. "That's stealing."

"All the information in those files is on the public record as part of the bankruptcy. I'd've given them up any time the FBI asked."

"It's just so weird," she said. "I mean, they even gave me this phone number to call for help, in case you found out and threatened me or something."

"Did the woman from the U.S. Attorney's office say anything?"

"Not to me. She and that Mr. Cravens whispered a lot."

Irritation flickered in Congo's eyes. "Okay, look Muffie, I'm sorry you were dragged into this. Forget what I said about copying the files. You're not paid for that kind of nonsense. I'll have my lawyer call the U.S. Attorney's office and see if he can talk them into behaving like adults."

"I'm not scared," she insisted, and then complained, "I never get in on anything."

Congo relented with a conspiratorial wink. He went into his office to start through the messages and e-mails that had piled up while he had been out of the country. Two were from owl-eyed Oscar Reubens regarding his lease at Crestline Center. Congo called Karen Steele's number. His response was a three day old recording that she would be out of town. He frowned and went back to his mail.

Muffie buzzed his extension. "An Adrienne Palmer, Mr. Congo. She says she's returning your call."

27

The *Mandalay* restaurant's claim to fame and exorbitant prices was an outdoor terrace that looked across Palisades Park and the Coast Highway at the historic fishing pier and the crumbly cliffs that edged the Pacific. Adrienne Palmer held court in a magnificent rattan chair, watching foam-crested waves roll in without end. A simple black suit de-emphasized her figure. Pancake didn't quite fill the tiny facial lines that foretold her future.

"I used to come here when I needed to get away from Madison for a few hours," she said without looking up at Congo. "Now that he's gone I have to come here to get away from his memory."

Congo sat down opposite her. "I am sorry, Mrs. Palmer. We were all hoping your husband would recover."

Variable tint glasses screened the emotion in her eyes but couldn't keep her voice from cracking when she said, "apparently." She repeated the word, recovering some composure, "the bullet severed something called a femoral artery."

"Then he was shot in the leg," Congo realized.

"What's this about, John? The hurried meeting. Suddenly you have to see me."

"May I speak frankly, Mrs. Palmer?"

"I wish you would."

"You came for the same reason I invited you," he said. "Neither of us believes your husband was shot by accident."

Her mouth tightened. "Do you know something?"

"The problem is that I don't, and I need to."

"Be candid with me, John. I was the one who nagged Madison into that stupid hunting trip."

"Did anyone put you up to it?"

"Put me up to it?"

"Mention that it would be a good idea. Hillman? Easter? Any of the Athens crowd?"

A pitying smile made short work of his theory. She took a sip from her teacup and put it down carefully, as if it were a thousand year old museum piece.

"Madison is a moody sort. One of his favorites is what I call his Daniel Webster mood. The invincible lawyer, ready to take on the devil if need be. He's easier to live with if I let a little air out of his balloon. He got into that mood over the lawsuit he planned to file against Athens. I knew he was deathly afraid of guns, so I nagged him about facing his fear and going on the hunting trip. I just wanted to remind him he had his share of human weaknesses. Now I feel like I sent him to die."

She stared into the distance, as if hoping the ocean breeze that teased her hair might be bringing forgiveness. A lunch crowd was beginning to gather at the tables around them. Congo waved off an approaching waitress.

"The lawsuit," he ventured, "what brought it on?"

"I think you know."

"If I knew," Congo said impatiently, "I wouldn't be going to all this trouble to ask."

She moved her shoulders in a vague shrug. "All he told me was that another attorney called him with a potential witness against Athens, and that you knew more than you had let on."

"Who was the attorney?"

"I don't know."

"Who was the witness?"

"Madison wouldn't say."

"Royce Hillman did, when he put you up to that little soap opera down in Mexico."

Color came to her cheeks. "Madison was getting in over his head. It's one thing to nit-pick contracts and represent your rich friends in petty squabbles. It's quite another to take on Royce Hillman. Madison's well off, but not wealthy. The fight would break him financially. Losing would break him emotionally. I tried to warn him, but he wouldn't listen."

"What did Hillman tell you?"

"He wanted to drive a wedge between you and Madison. He said you put Madison up to suing. That you provided the witness to support his claim."

"Who was the witness?"

She considered him carefully, studying his face for any sign the question was not completely candid. "Catherine Carson," she said in a voice haunted by the specter of front page scandal.

"Thank you," Congo said.

She was still, visibly expectant, waiting for him to say more. When he didn't she spoke softly and earnestly.

"I brought my husband's body back yesterday. I'm going to bury him tomorrow. I agreed to meet you today because I thought you might at least have the decency to tell me what really happened."

A helpless smile was all Congo had to offer. "Write me off as a bad person. You won't be far wrong."

She stood without excusing herself and left, her carriage erect but her pace measured under a burden of sadness. Congo made several calls on his cell phone and then flagged down a waitress. He had finished a lunch of spring rolls and rice by the time the hostess escorted China Doll Carson to his table. He stood graciously.

"Thank you for coming, Catherine."

She smiled while the hostess installed her in the rattan chair Adrienne Palmer had vacated, tucking her purse on the cushion beside her rather than placing it on the floor. The hostess left and Congo sat down.

"I mean you no harm," he said.

She kept a hand on the purse. Her stylish jacket was too heavy for the afternoon's warmth. Her hair had been re-done to fall straight, covering her cheeks and curving inward at her jaw where a silk scarf shimmered in a variety of hues. Her sunglasses were large, and darker than the day required. She looked like a fugitive.

"You can't be happy with me," she said.

"Adrienne Palmer wanted to know why her husband was shot. I didn't dare tell her for fear of winding up in Federal prison."

Catherine looked away into the park toward the elderly chess players and the wandering homeless.

"Am I to blame for that?" A quiver of uncertainty made the question genuine, not the product of her years as an actress.

"You told Madison Palmer that you rigged the Crestline Bankruptcy in my favor after Royce Hillman demanded you rig it in his."

Silence hung between them. The breeze ruffled napkins. Snippets of conversation drifted from nearby tables. She faced Congo again, her eyes an enigma behind the sunglasses.

"The truth wasn't going to stay hidden forever."

"How did you hook up with Palmer? Was he another client?"

"My lawyer knew him. Or at least knew he owned an interest in the Elysian Hotel and had a lot to lose."

"Madison Palmer was a stuffed shirt who saw his chance to be taken seriously. He was going to publicize the whole mess in a lawsuit and spoil Royce Hillman's chances of putting together the Athens deal."

"I'm afraid the cat's out of the bag, John," she said softly. "The FBI knows too."

"Why, Catherine? Was it that important to even the score against Hillman?"

Her face tightened with urgency. "This isn't about payback. It's about protecting ourselves. Royce had Palmer shot, didn't he?"

"I don't know," Congo said, adding, "maybe," when she wrinkled her mouth at him and conceding, "probably," when that didn't satisfy her.

"Royce Hillman isn't finished with us," she said. "We know too much, and he knows we know it."

Congo studied his reflection in her sunglasses. "Is that why you came, Catherine? To recruit me for your little crusade?"

"We need each other," she insisted. "If we're going to survive."

"It won't work," Congo said.

"I can't do it on my own."

He shook his head. She gathered her purse and stood to leave.

"Sit down," he ordered. "You need to hear this."

Indignation stiffened her, but uncertainty stifled any outburst. She sat at the front edge of her chair.

"It won't work," Congo said, "because you have no evidence of crime or tort. Remember, Hillman thought you were going to influence the Judge on his behalf. He tried to take advantage of that by submitting a low bid. I didn't know you were stacking the deck in my favor, so I entered a high bid. Whatever the Judge's reasons, when he found in my favor, he chose the best offer, which he was duty bound to do in any case."

"He acted under threat of exposure of unlawful activity."

"It was illegal for you to make a threat against him," Congo said, "but it wasn't illegal for him to receive it."

"He was legally bound to report it," she said. "At least according to my attorney."

"Lapse of judgment," Congo said. "Your little black book, even if it became public, wouldn't get him any more than a brief suspension and some counseling."

"Not what my attorney said," she retorted. "And not what Madison Palmer said."

"Because you told them that you influenced the Judge to take an inferior offer. As soon as the arithmetic becomes public, and the FBI has it by now, the whole case will evaporate."

Her composure began to disintegrate under visible disappointment and fatigue. She sagged back in her chair.

"Even if a criminal case existed," Congo went on, "I seriously doubt that it would be prosecuted. If the Judge were convicted of wrongdoing in any bankruptcy case, every bankruptcy he ever tried would come into question. Losers would come out of the woodwork, petitioning to re-open. It would be a can of worms for the court."

"Do you think you've won?" she asked. "Do you think you'll just be able to walk away?"

"Walking away is not my idea of victory," Congo said. "I came to L.A. to turn my life around. I'm not just looking for ways to beat the rap."

"Are you hoping I'll keep my mouth shut?"

"I'm telling you that your hope of trading what you know about the Crestline Bankruptcy for leniency in your own case is gone. Talk to your attorney. I think he'll tell you that same thing."

A waitress arrived with a menu. Catherine stood, waving it away, and left. The grace that had carried her down countless fashion show runways was a forlorn shadow of itself.

Congo paid his check and went out to retrieve his Porsche. There was a small envelope taped to the steering wheel. The driver's license inside belonged to Karen Steele. The accompanying note had come from a laser printer.

Accrued interest and fees have brought your debt to $100,000. Used $50 bills. Unmarked. No consecutive serial numbers. Delivery instructions will follow. This is a private matter. Handle it personally. Contact no one.

Congo glanced around. He was alone in a parking lot full of empty cars. He looked at Karen's license, at her photograph. His hand trembled.

"Shit," he said under his breath.

28

Rachel Krebs was allotted a small workstation in Hillman Management's accounting department. Stacks of invoices crowded the desk space around a monitor and keyboard. Ring binders overflowed the shelves. On those she had propped a stuffed cartoon cat to watch over her. Her space was private only in the sense that its location against the back wall prevented nearby co-workers from looking in.

"You shouldn't have come here," she told Congo in an angry whisper.

"Sit down, Rachel. Please. I won't be long. I promise."

"No," she declared. "I'm tired of being pushed around by people who think they're important. I'm tired of being patted on the head like some stupid puppy."

"Rachel, please, I'm not trying to—"

"I photocopied that list of owners for you," she reminded him. "This isn't a very nice way to thank me."

He acknowledged his imposition with a contrite nod.

"Tell me what you want," she said.

He indicated the chair.

"Right now," she insisted. "Not when you feel like you're in control. Tell me. Or go away. Or I'll call security."

Hot eyes and compressed lips left no doubt of her determination. Congo held up both hands in a gesture of surrender.

"I just need to know if you processed a check for $100,000 today."

Astonishment opened her mouth. No words came out.

"It would have been a manual request," Congo said. "Probably made out to cash."

"Who told you?" she demanded in a low voice indignant over breach of confidentiality.

"Who signed the request? Hillman or Easter?"

"The new controller." Superior knowledge squared her shoulders.

"Who signed the check?"

"Mr. Hillman has to sign any check over $50,000."

Hillman's name came out with enough disgust to suggest festering resentment. Shrewdness lit Congo's eyes.

"How are you and Lee getting along?"

"Lee was just an outlet for suppressed emotions," she informed him. "I'm getting in touch with those feelings so I can deal with them in a healthy way."

"Is your company medical plan paying for counseling?"

"Yes."

Congo wished her well, found his way back to the lobby and started down the executive corridor, opening doors as he went, glancing inside and closing each without apology to the people upon whom he intruded until he found Royce Hillman seated in a conference room.

The executive was addressing a group of men in business attire. He looked up startled at Congo's entrance. Before the surprise could pass, Congo strode to his chair, leaned down and spoke quietly into his ear.

"Mr. Hillman, I suggest a short recess. You and I need to talk about the note you received."

Hillman brought his bulk out of the chair and directed a benevolent smile at the assembled group.

"I am sorry. Something urgent has come up. We're about due for a break. Let's take fifteen minutes."

Hillman led Congo out of the room and lumbered down the hall. His office was a spacious corner looking north and west through tall windows. Smog hung like corruption in the stagnant air outside, shrouding the San Gabriel Mountains in a brown haze and making the Pacific Ocean seem distant and dirty. Hillman closed the door and installed himself in his high-backed leather swivel chair, where he could confront Congo from behind the authority of his massive desk.

"Now, suppose you tell me about this note," he demanded in a voice full of dire consequences.

Congo set the ransom note he had received on the desk. Hillman put on a pair of spectacles and peered at it. He removed the spectacles and peered at Congo from behind the pads of fat that compressed and protected his eyes.

"What's your game?"

"Not mine," Congo said, appropriating a chair in front of the desk. "It started as yours. Now it belongs to Gregory Demirjian."

"Demirjian?"

"My note mentions a debt. I expect yours did too. Abduction is a loan shark's tactic of last recourse."

"That's hardly sufficient basis to conclude that—"

"You left him no choice."

Color rose in Hillman's face. "Now see here, Congo, you can't blame me for this."

"You're the idiot who put Raymond's game into the Elysian. When Raymond was killed, Demirjian lost both money and face. Neither you nor I could make good his losses. If we had paid, he'd've shaken us down forever. And he can't afford to let the debt go. If we get away with stiffing him, everyone will try. You put him into Catch 22."

"Drivel!" Hillman snapped.

"You've heard of chaos theory?" Congo asked.

"The butterfly effect? Of course. What of it?"

"You, Mr. Hillman, are the butterfly. The police came to you for a help running a sting against the Armenian mafia. You saw it as a nice little scare for the owners of the Elysian. Something to bump them toward a secure sounding deal like Athens. You set off a chain reaction of unintended consequences. And there's no guarantee we've seen the last of them."

Hillman was visibly annoyed at being lectured. "Why kidnap Karen?"

"Demirjian's no fool," Congo said. "He had us watched, looking for any weakness. His people saw both of us talking to Karen repeatedly. She became the logical fulcrum to give him leverage against us."

The executive considered Congo. "How do I know this isn't some confidence trick you've cooked up to try to frustrate the Athens initiative?"

"Believe me or call the police," Congo said. "Those are the only real options you have."

Hillman squirmed without getting comfortable. "This may not be the right time to involve the police. If this man Demirjian is responsible, he can be dealt with after Karen is safely away from him."

"For once we agree," Congo said.

"What are your plans?" Hillman asked.

Congo stood and plucked his note off the desk. "This says to wait for instructions. I haven't received any."

"But you do plan to pay?"

"I need to be sure you're going to pay. It wouldn't be good if one of us anted up and the other brought in the police."

"I see no option other than payment," Hillman said. "At least for the present."

"I'm not questioning your decision, Mr. Hillman. I just need to know that it's final. That you mean to go through with it."

The executive leaned back in his swivel chair. "There is one thing you need to understand, John. Karen was never for you. If she ever forms another serious relationship, it will be with a business leader. Someone she can look up to. A father figure for those boys of hers. You see, she understands one thing you don't seem to have grasped. Modern business is natural selection in its purest form. Survival of the fittest."

"Don't be too quick to invoke the law of the jungle," Congo warned. "It's not a pleasant place. I've been there. You wouldn't like it."

"It's just a bit of paternal advice," Hillman said. "You'll call me when you've received your instructions?"

"You'll hear about it before I transfer a nickel," Congo promised. "Thank you for your time, Mr. Hillman."

"I wish you'd call me Royce."

Congo went out of the office. He rode the elevator to the garage where he found that Hillman and Easter had reserved parking stalls on the first level. Easter's car was a Lexus sedan, appropriately down market from Hillman's Bentley. Congo retrieved his Porsche and drove back to his own building.

"Hi Muffie," he said cheerfully. "Do the Feds have us surrounded yet?"

"I think they tapped the phones," she said. "Enrico asked a lot of questions to confirm who had what extension. And he wants me to get him into the computer system so he can check and see if there are any more bankruptcy files besides what I gave him."

"Set it up for this afternoon. Les and I will be out of here by four."

Congo went into his office and used the intercom to ask Abe Lester to join him. Lester came in carrying several sheets of fax paper and closed the door.

"I did what you told me. Called your lawyer and asked him to check on any real estate this guy Demirjian had owned and sold. So what the hell is it about?"

Congo told him.

"Jesus fucking Christ," Lester said. "Kidnapping is a Federal offense. You gotta turn that ransom note over."

"It's not a ransom note," Congo said. "Just instructions for payment of an unspecified obligation."

Lester waved his handful of faxes. "So what's this crap about?"

"How do you launder money?" Congo asked.

"You think Demirjian's been phonying up real estate transactions?"

"It's a generic scam. Demirjian buys property on the cheap, holds it ' enough to qualify for capital gains treatment on the taxes and suddenly a ' appears to take it off his hands at an obscene profit."

"The buyer being Demirjian himself," Lester supplied, "or at least offshore corporation he's been dropping his ill-gotten gains into."

"Putting the money into Demirjian's US account," Congo concluded, "looking squeaky clean. And leaving him in control of the property."

Worry darkened Lester's face. "You think he's using one of these places to hold the Steele broad."

"Unless you have a better idea."

"So what do you do? Go door knocking? Excuse me, sir; are there any kidnap victims at this address?"

"Easter will make Hillman's payment tonight. I'll follow Easter then follow the pick-up man. That should put me in the neighborhood, but it could get dicey from there. I need to be sure of the location."

"How do you know what Hillman's going to do?"

"He didn't ask me how I thought the payoff would work. If he wasn't curious, it means he already had his instructions. Demirjian wouldn't give him time to think, so it's tonight. And Hillman isn't the type to do his own dirty work."

Lester was dubious. "Even if you luck out and pull it off, the Steele broad won't be impressed. Women aren't looking for white knights. They're looking for a man they can share life with. I mean what's she going to do? Sit around all day polishing your armor?"

Congo shook his head. "Karen was always out of reach. It just took me awhile to figure it out. This is to get Demirjian out of my rear view."

"Yeah, right," Lester said. "Seriously, John, they got cops in this town."

Congo's face hardened at mention of the police. He put a plastic-wrapped cell phone on the desk.

"Prepaid. Don't leave any prints on it. Trash it when you're done."

"Done with what?"

"Find an internet café," Congo instructed. "Log on to a satellite mapping site and plug those addresses in. I'll call you when I have an approximate location. You can direct me from there."

"What happened to going straight?" Lester asked.

"Not now, Les."

"Never mind the Steele broad," Lester said. "Never mind you're going up against this Demirjian outnumbered and outgunned. This ain't about that shit. This is about you. This is about who you really are. Do you really want to turn it around and start doing things right or are you going to spend the rest of your life cutting corners?"

"We need to be out of here by four so Muffie can let the Feds in to bug the place," Congo said.

29

Harbingers of changing weather pursued Congo on the drive home. Chill wind gusted off the Pacific, scouring the smog out of the Los Angeles basin, sweeping in great billows of cumulus that turned the winding streets of Los Feliz into a manic-depressive pattern of brilliant sun and brooding shadows. Congo put his Porsche in the garage, collected his armored vest and the M-16 assault rifle he and Clint Phillips had taken from Raymond Stepanian's nephews and locked both into the trunk of the Valiant. He backed the car out into random drops of rain fell and drove downtown.

The garage under Hillman's office building was constructed with a single exit so that one minimum wage attendant could collect payment from departing cars. The pedestrian exit from the building lobby was around the corner. Only a few strategic street parking spots allowed a simultaneous view of both. Congo circled the block several times before he was able to claim one.

The clouds darkened and the rain intensified, pelting pedestrians and sheeting the sidewalks. Rush hour traffic turned streets into rivers of frayed nerves and angry horns. Easter emerged from the lobby carrying an attaché case and an umbrella and boarded the first in a line of taxis. Congo started the Valiant.

Traffic was a slow-moving prison. The cab led Congo to Sepulveda and they joined a fitful convoy making its way up and over the Santa Monicas and down into an older area of the San Fernando Valley. The taxi's first destination was a strip mall. Easter got out, huddled beneath his umbrella, and hurried into a storefront florist's shop. Cars went by out on the boulevard, spraying water and spearing the gathering gloom with their headlight beams. Easter returned to the cab clutching his umbrella, his attaché case and a florist's box in a clumsy jumble. Congo gave the vehicle more room on less traveled side streets and parked well back when it drew up to the gate of a small cemetery.

Easter made his way into the cemetery alone, struggling to keep his umbrella oriented against the wind and rain, searching among the grave markers, visibly unsure of his destination. He had left the attaché case behind, and carried only the florist's box. At length he found an upright stone, opened the box and set his flower arrangement against the granite. The box and lid blew away. Easter hastened back to the taxi, carrying only the umbrella. Congo stayed put when the taxi carried Easter away.

"Nice touch, Mr. Demirjian," he said. "Dead witnesses tell no tales."

Congo used a second prepaid cell phone to dial the number he had given Abe Lester.

"John, is that you? Jesus fucking Christ. I'd given you up for dead."

"Not yet," Congo said. "But there is a cemetery handy."

"Where the hell are you?"

"I followed Easter out to the Valley. He left the money in a graveyard."

"Just left it?"

"The Valley is tent city for middle-class nomads. Only the dead stay behind. After a while, there's no one left to visit them. Particularly in this weather."

"John, this storm is no fluke, you know. Demirjian and anyone else who watched the news knew it was coming. I mean, Christ. Demirjian picks the time. He picks the place. He even picks the weather. He's got everything going for him. You got nothing going for you."

"You're my edge, Les. Tell me what property Demirjian has within five miles of here." Congo gave him the cross streets.

"There's a shitload," Lester came back. "I count eight, nine, three more makes a dozen, call it fourteen in all."

"Bank night," Congo exulted. "What's the—"

Lights appeared on the street fronting the cemetery.

"Company, Les. Call you later." Congo cut the connection.

The car was a ten year old Corolla, well-kept, with no damage to mark it for witnesses, generic enough to blend in anywhere. It circled the cemetery once and went on its way. Congo was well back up a boulevard and outside its search range.

Time passed.

Brake lights glowed and a car stopped at the wrought iron arch over the cemetery entrance. The car was low and screened by intervening vehicles. The figure that rose from the passenger side appeared to be a woman. Congo cursed his view.

Dusk and downpour reduced the woman to a shadow. An umbrella hid her face. A large bag hung from her shoulder. She fought the blustery wind into the cemetery, surer of her direction than Easter had been. When she returned, her shoulder bag appeared bulkier and heavier. Congo brought the Valiant to life.

The woman's transportation proved to be the red Trans-Am from which Raymond Stepanian's nephews had tried to ambush Congo and Clint Phillips. It led

Congo to a taxi stand. The woman got out. Her bag had lost its bulk and its weight. The Trans-Am hovered protectively until she was safely in a cab and on her way. Congo stayed with the Trans-Am.

The trip lasted less than a mile. The Trans-Am parked next to a temporary hurricane fence thrown up around a block of abandoned houses. A street lamp threw light on a sign announcing the coming of an apartment complex. The remainder of the area was either abandoned homes or fenced-off apartment foundations being excavated. Urban renewal had come to the suburbs, creating a temporary enclave of empty residences rendered invisible by surrounding construction. Congo shut down the Valiant at the curb.

It was Raymond Stepanian's nephew, Nicky, who got out of the Trans-Am. He had a package under his arm, briefly visible in the glow of the interior light before he closed and locked the door. The cast of a street lamp showed him slipping through a breach in the hurricane fence and making directly for the front door of one of the abandoned houses. It opened as he approached and he disappeared inside. No light escaped. Congo retrieved his cell phone and pressed out Lester's number.

"John?" Lester asked. "What the hell is going on?"

Congo gave him the closest cross streets. "What does Demirjian have near here?"

"Christ, there's one, two, three of them. One is only half a block north of you."

"That looks right."

"Hey, John, we had, like, two hours to throw this list together. No way is it complete."

"No worries, Les. They parked a nice red car in front to mark the place."

"Sucker play," was Lester's immediate response.

"I don't think so. This whole thing has gone too smoothly to be a first run. Demirjian has used this template before. And when something works, people tend to stick with it, mistakes and all."

"How many guys you figure Demirjian has with him?" Lester asked.

"I'll tell you when I get back," Congo promised.

"Are you coming back, John? Or have you finally lost it?"

"Lost what?"

"I'm talking death wish. Hillman's going to take the hotel and bankrupt Crestline again and let the air out of your big dream. You finally figured out you got no shot with the Steele broad. So you're going out in a blaze of glory. Is that it?"

"Just stay where you are for the next half hour," Congo instructed. "Make sure you have witnesses."

"John—"

Congo cut the connection.

"Okay, genius," he said to himself. "So let's say you get lucky and pull this off. How the hell do you get out of here?"

He moved the Valiant to a nearby street that pointed toward Sepulveda, visible in the distance as a rain-blurred ribbon of moving lights. The street was empty, stealth unnecessary. He stripped off his suit coat, opened the trunk, put on his armored vest and replaced the coat. Tucking the assault rifle under his arm, he closed the trunk and set off.

Wind billowed his coat and strafed him with rain. His shoes sloshed in puddles and squished in mud as he moved carefully among the litter of broken cinder block and lumber scraps. He peered into the Trans-Am to be sure it was empty.

The fence where Nicky had gone through was still sprung far enough to pass Congo's trim frame. The house that had swallowed Stepanian's nephew was a single story ranch. Bits of light leaked from knotholes and cracks where the windows had been boarded against trespass. Wooden fencing blocked access to the rear yard. Congo tested the front door knob, found it secured.

The only other entry was a door leading in from the dark interior of a carport, visible only as slivers of light leaking out where the weather stripping had rotted. Congo moved under the cover. He stopped and removed his glasses, using a handkerchief to wipe rain and mist from the lenses.

Rain beat on the roof of the carport and gurgled in the downspouts. Voices were audible through the walls.

"There wasn't no trouble, Uncle Gregory," Nicky insisted. "I done just like you told me. I drove Aunt Rae out there and put her in a cab afterward and made sure no one followed her or nothing and then came straight here. There wasn't no trouble."

"I'm not criticizing you, my boy," Demirjian said in a fatherly wheeze. "I am simply being diligent. We must always be alert for trouble."

"Okay, Uncle Gregory," Congo said under his breath, "if you're looking for trouble, you're looking in the right place."

He set the assault rifle to fire semi-automatic, lifted his leg and drove his foot against the door with all his strength.

30

The impact of Congo's kick was enough to splinter the jamb but not much more. The door pivoted inward only a foot before it scraped to a stop. Light flooded out to reveal a barricade of trash littering a scaly linoleum floor. Congo drove his shoulder against the wood, forcing his way inside.

Four men sat around a card table. Indignation brought Gregory Demirjian to his feet. His grand-nephew Nicky jerked erect, brimming with juvenile hostility. The tall east European called Eddie rose smoothly, shifting his eyes, sizing up the threat. His partner Arthur came up snatching an automatic from his belt. Congo snapped the assault rifle to his shoulder and triggered a single round.

The noise was savage in the confined space, reverberating off the walls and echoing away into the dark recesses of the house. The bullet took Arthur in the chest, lifting his coat as it tore out through his back and raising dust when it punched through the wall behind him. Tension evaporated from his body. The automatic slipped from his limp fingers. He followed it to the carpet, sagging straight down as his knees buckled and then pitching forward to a solid face plant.

Eddie bent swiftly into a corner of the room. He came up with Karen Steele in front of him as a shield, his fingers wound into her hair.

Duct tape covered her mouth. Her hands were behind her, probably bound together. What had been a stylish pant suit hung limp. Stray tendrils drooped over a grimy face. Her gaze riveted on Congo and her eyes filled with terror.

Congo's veneer was gone, replaced by animal tension. Rain had left his clothing sodden and shapeless. His armored vest made him hulking, anthropoid. He shifted the muzzle of the assault rifle, as if probing for another target.

Eddie put the point of a tactical knife to Karen's throat. "Rifle on the counter," he told Congo. "Nice and easy."

The counter was actually a filthy breakfast bar that separated the gutted kitchen where Congo stood from the family room that held the others. The only light came from the family room, from a gas camping lantern hung from dead electrical wires where a ceiling fixture had been ripped out. Congo eased around the end of the breakfast bar and into the family room.

"Hollywood," he said, "is about twenty miles down the road."

157

The acrid residue of burnt nitro powder accented air stale with the odor of the recently eaten fast food. Wrappers still littered the card table, pushed aside to make room for a large waterproof refrigerator bag and sheaves of currency. Demirjian came around the table to stand protectively in front of the money, tugging the sleeves of his suit coat down over starched cuffs until only a hint of gold links shimmered in the lantern light.

"Mr. Congo," he began in a strict voice, but stopped when Arthur twitched on the carpet.

Congo glanced down. "That's a sucking chest wound. If it's not blocked front and back, enough air will get into his chest cavity to collapse his lungs and he'll die."

Eddie eyed his partner anxiously. "That's straight," he agreed.

"Nicky," Congo snapped, "take two of those aluminum foil food wrappers and close both wounds, entry and exit. Hold them down firmly enough for a tight seal."

"Fuck you," Nicky shot back. He glanced at the automatic Arthur had dropped.

"And kick that pistol away," Congo added.

Nicky repeated himself.

Demirjian spoke softly. "Do as he says, my boy."

Nicky's upper lip curled in rebellion.

Demirjian patted his arm. "It's all right. Eddie and I will deal with this situation."

Nicky launched the automatic across the room with a vicious kick, retrieved two food wrappers and knelt beside Arthur. A smile fixed itself on Demirjian's full lips and managed to cling there while he spoke.

"You must be reasonable, Mr. Congo. Whatever your original intentions in finding your way here, you have failed. We need to resolve this matter without further violence."

"If I had anything against violence," Congo said, "I wouldn't have shot Arthur. And if you had anything against it, you wouldn't be snatching women off the street."

Karen stood with her head at an awkward angle to minimize the pressure of Eddie's hold. Fear was draining from her eyes, replaced by questions she was powerless to articulate as she looked from Congo to Demirjian.

"You forced me to this resort," Demirjian insisted. "I gave you every opportunity to pay. I gave you every opportunity to make reasonable counter proposals.

But instead of negotiating in good faith, you come here with a rifle and shoot a member of my family in cold blood."

"There's nothing remotely cold about my blood," Congo warned.

"Come, now. You are a business man. Such threats are beneath you."

"I'm not spending the rest of my life checking my rear view for you and your third world mafia. I came here to make sure you understood that."

"I think not, Mr. Congo. You did not come here to see me for the simple reason that you had no assurance I would be here."

"Of course you'd be here," Congo retorted. "You came in person to try to shake me down for the money you loaned to Raymond. You came in person when I asked for a meeting. You're a control freak. If money was changing hands, you'd be here to receive it. And you'd have the merchandise where you could keep an eye on it."

Demirjian conceded Congo's logic with a smirk. "Perhaps we should consult Mrs. Steele?"

She squirmed a bit and her mouth tried to move under the tape. Congo winked at her.

"Okay. Fine. Turn her loose. We'll all have a nice chat."

"I cannot permit myself to be humiliated," Demirjian said in an asthmatic purr. "I have already explained to you that credibility is everything to a man in my business."

"You're out of business," Congo said. "You've just extorted a hundred thousand dollars from Royce Hillman. Hillman can't afford to be humiliated any more than you can. The difference is that his contributions helped elect the Prosecutor. He uses the police like chess pieces. As soon as Mrs. Steele is recovered, dead or alive, he'll have an arrest warrant out for you. The only reason I didn't shoot you outright is that Hillman will make sure that you're through in L.A."

Demirjian rippled impatient fingers against his trouser leg. "Eddie," he said.

Eddie forced Karen forward. Her face contorted in pain. Eddie brought her to where Demirjian stood. He measured Congo with contemptuous eyes.

"We know your steroid is dead. That means you came alone."

"Not entirely." Congo moved the muzzle of the rifle.

"You won't shoot," Eddie said. "You might hit the broad."

"You're too big to hide behind her."

"Rifle," Eddie said. "Give it over."

Demirjian held out a plump hand.

Congo eyed the two men who confronted him. They stood almost shoulder to shoulder, a scant five feet away. A smile spread across his face.

"All right," he said. "You want it, here it is."

He triggered another round.

The bullet passed head-high through the narrow space between Demirjian and Eddie. The muzzle blast hit sensitive ear drums and wrenched involuntary screams from both men. Demirjian recoiled in agony, stumbling over a chair. Eddie released Karen to reach instinctively for his ear. Karen staggered sideways, disoriented by the blast, unable to scream because of the tape. Congo seized her arm and yanked her away from Eddie.

"Behind me!" he yelled. "Go behind me!"

She twisted out of his grasp, moving erratically, stumbling as if circulation had not yet fully returned to her legs, clumsy with her hands fastened behind her. Eddie took half a step toward her and stopped when Congo swung the rifle to point at his face.

"Come ahead," Congo taunted. "I've still got plenty of aggression to work off."

Eddie licked his lips, didn't move.

Karen fled too quickly into the kitchen, losing her footing in the litter on the floor.

"Out the door," Congo instructed. "You'll be in a carport. Follow the driveway to the street. The fence is open there."

Congo backed slowly into the kitchen as Karen scrambled up and found her way out.

"Face down on the floor," he told the men in the room. "Stay there for five minutes. You won't get hurt."

Demirjian complied reluctantly, made awkward by his ample stomach. Eddie followed his example. Nicky glanced at Arthur. Congo shook his head.

"Not you. Just keep your head down." He stepped out into the carport and sprinted for the fence.

Karen was squeezing through to the street. The light in the house went out. Congo flipped the M-16's selector switch, shouldered the rifle and spread half a dozen shots chest high into the outer wall of the kitchen, full automatic.

Karen spilled through the fence and into a large puddle. Congo stepped through and hauled her up by one arm. He hurried her along the street through a minefield of rubbish.

"Move, damn it! I can't carry you."

She struggled, holding back, jerking from one side to the other, trying to break free, apparently as afraid of him as she was of any danger behind them. He was able to move her only because she seemed determined to keep her feet under her. He hauled her around the corner and shoved her against the Valiant.

Rain pelted them both.

She screamed when he ripped the tape from her mouth. He unlocked the driver's door, pushed her in, tossed the rifle into the rear foot well and shoved her over as he got behind the wheel.

"God, my ear!" she all but yelled at him as he sprayed gravel pulling away from the margin of the road.

"You're still alive," he said, snapping on the high beams.

"You just shot that man."

"That still leaves you one up on me."

"What—what are you talking about?"

"Raymond Stepanian and Madison Palmer."

She stared without comprehension, her face pale and blank in the sodium lights of passing intersections. Congo gave her an angry glance.

"Well, it was your crazy scheme that killed them, wasn't it?"

31

Congo found a commercial thoroughfare where a robust traffic flow offered concealment and protection. He glanced at Karen, pressed against the passenger door, as far from him as the confines of the car would allow.

"Are you all right?" he asked.

She didn't acknowledge him, not even a look.

"Come on, Karen. Talk to me. I need to know if you're okay. I mean, do we need to find you some medical attention?"

"No," she snapped.

"I'm just trying to help."

Discomfort made her squirm. "I really would like to get these wires off my wrists."

"Yeah. Sure. Give me a minute."

A strip mall appeared on the right. Several frontages had gone dark for the night. Congo found a secluded corner in the parking lot and shut down the Valiant.

Karen turned her back to him. Her wrists had been fastened with heavy gauge electrical wire. As soon as he had twisted it off, she began to rub circulation back into her wrists and hands.

Congo struggled out of his sodden coat and peeled off his armored vest. Karen watched him stow the vest behind the seat, on top of the rifle, and drape the coat to cover both.

"How did you find me?" she asked.

He fished out his wallet and found her drivers' license and the ransom note. She unfolded the note and read it by the boulevard lights once he had the Valiant back in traffic.

"That," he said, "is the danger of over-reaching. Demirjian sent one of those to me and one to Hillman. I followed Hillman's ransom payment."

"Life lessons from the school of hard knocks." She tucked the note and license into a jacket pocket. "You're only reformed when it's convenient."

She found an old fashioned scrunchy in another pocket, corralled as much of her hair as she could and fastened it behind her head. Weariness infiltrated Congo's voice, notice that his adrenaline was draining away.

"I guess I should have seen it when Hillman introduced us at the golf course," he said.

"Seen what?"

"I told Hillman and Easter that I'd been a gambler. They had visions of organized crime and called the boss to come check me out."

"The boss?"

"Hillman didn't think up the Athens deal," Congo said. "He hasn't the imagination or the motivation."

"Royce," she retorted, "is Athens."

"He's a stuffed shirt who gets his jollies pushing people around and popping off about leadership. But his management business gave him access to the owners of major properties. So you recruited him to front Athens."

"I recruited him?" Mocking laughter lay just beneath her words.

"It was Adrienne Palmer's play in Mexico that really gave you away," Congo said. "To make it work, Adrienne needed to have me to herself. When you blew off the invitation to my bungalow, you knew I'd be alone. And you were the only one who knew. No one else could have cued Adrienne."

"John, don't you think you're letting your imagination run away with you?"

"It's not just Mexico," he said. "Hillman raised a hundred thousand dollar ransom and didn't tell the police. He wouldn't have done that for a good little vice president. He bailed you out because you're the engine driving Athens. He's afraid he can't pull it off without you."

Karen turned the mirror. She grimaced at her reflection, found a small packet of tissues in the glove box and set to work cleaning her face. Congo fidgeted at her silence.

"Hillman's mistakes are compounding themselves," Congo said. "He tried to use China Doll Carson to rig the Crestline bankruptcy so he could become a shareholder in the Elysian Hotel. When that failed, he let a dice game into the hotel to spook the legitimate owners so they'd be receptive to the Athens deal. That got Demirjian's nephew killed and you kidnapped. Hillman also had China Doll Carson arrested to silence her. That backfired when Carson went to Madison Palmer with her story, so Hillman had Palmer shot before Palmer could take Hillman's shenanigans public in a lawsuit."

"Royce doesn't kill people," she said without taking her attention from the mirror and her efforts to repair her appearance. "It isn't his style."

"The bullet may have been meant to immobilize Palmer in Mexico until after the shareholders' vote," Congo conceded. "Palmer's dying created more problems than it solved."

Karen let out an exasperated sigh. "Would you like to know how Athens really came to be? Or are you happier with your little fantasy?"

"I couldn't be more curious," Congo admitted.

"There was nothing dark or sinister about it. Accumulating separate pieces of commercial property into a single investment portfolio is common practice. Insurance companies and syndication firms do it all the time."

They crested the Santa Monicas and started down into the Los Angeles basin, a throbbing network of lights spreading endlessly beneath a malignant overcast, blurred by the rain swept windshield and by the metronome passing of the wipers.

"There's your empire," Congo said. "It's devoured everyone who's tried to rule it."

"Athens isn't about ruling. It's about pulling together diverse properties into a whole that is greater than the sum of the parts."

"That theory works for insurers and syndicators," Congo said, "for the same reason bundling games of chance works for a casino. The casino is rich enough to stand a few losses and the house percentage favors them over the long haul."

"John, please, I didn't just dream up Athens on the spur of the moment. I've talked to a lot of property owners over the years. People I've negotiated leases for. They want the strength and security of association. They just don't know how to enable it. They need a spark of creativity to get the process going."

"It's not lack of creativity that's stopping them," Congo said. "It's common sense. Without the financial staying power of a large corporation behind you, your first mis-step is your last."

She ran out of tissues and wadded the packet in frustration. "You don't want to understand, do you?"

"I understand risk," Congo said. "You are going into the Athens deal with no safety net. Every risk that goes bad will require a more desperate risk to correct it. It's already started to catch up with you. Tonight was just the beginning."

"What do you suggest?"

"Shut down Athens," he said. "Now. Before anyone else gets hurt."

"If you're frightened, why don't you sell your shares in the Elysian? Buy something safe?"

"And give up everything I've worked for?" he asked.

"If you won't give up your dream, why should I give up mine?"

Congo opened his mouth to protest but thought better of the idea.

"We're all prisoners of our desires," she said. "They shape us. They define who we are. They keep us going when everything around us is falling apart."

"Two caged animals in one old car," he said.

They rode awhile in silence, carried along in the relentless flow of L.A. traffic.

"Drop me at my office," she said. "I keep a change of outfit there."

"Are you sure you'll be okay on your own? The last two days can't have been easy."

"That shouldn't matter to you," she said.

"It shouldn't," he agreed. "But it does."

She studied his profile in the passing lights and her voice softened. "Not what I would have expected from a steely-eyed professional gambler."

"What I know and what I feel are two different things," he said. "I'll just have to deal with that. So will you."

"What do you know about my feelings?"

"You made your decision back in the parking lot," he said. "The smart move was for you to bail out of the car while I was wrestling my coat off and make a run for the nearest open store. You stayed."

"I am who I am," she warned. "I wouldn't change to save my marriage and I have no plans to change now."

"I'm not looking for an angel. I've never met anyone who wasn't trying to get an edge on. I'm not sure such people exist, and I'm damned sure I wouldn't know how to act if I ran across one."

"It's not about acting. It's about being genuine. It's about finding the courage to step out from behind the poker face and be the person you really are."

"I'm not stepping out from behind my poker face," Congo said, "any more than you're stepping out from behind your cheerleader smile. Learned behavior is as much a part of our persona as anything else."

She put up her hands. "Truce," she said. "No more drugstore psychiatry. From either of us."

"Okay," Congo said. "But there is one thing you need to do. Call Hillman. Tell him you're free, but don't give him any details. Just tell him he has to get an arrest warrant issued for Gregory Demirjian tonight."

She nodded.

"No," he said. "Don't just blow me off. Demirjian is angry and he's dangerous. We're all in jeopardy until he's taken out of circulation. It doesn't matter what the charges are. The police have plenty on him. But Hillman has to move tonight. No matter how many favors he has to call in. You have to call him and insist."

"I will," she said. "You needn't fret."

"Only the paranoid survive," Congo said.

She gave him a worried glance. "Will you be attending the shareholder meeting?"

"What's the matter?" Congo asked. "Are you afraid I'll do the right thing for once in my life?"

32

"What's the point of going to this shareholders' meeting?" Abe Lester asked. "You already know how it's going to turn out."

"If it were just the vote, I'd stay home." Congo checked his reflection in the reception area relight.

"Well, if you're trying to impress the Steele broad you'd better lose the tie. And find a leather jacket. That suit's a nice tailoring job but it makes you look like a fossil. Also, clean shaves are out."

Congo winked at Muffie. "Did you call Hillman Management?"

"Mr. Easter was out so I left your message. You need fifteen minutes of his time before the meeting. You've re-thought things but you have a couple of questions."

"Thanks," Congo said. "Anything more from the Feds since they cancelled the bugging session?"

"Enrico called. The FBI doesn't have enough probable cause to continue the investigation."

"I guess there is some percentage in playing it straight," Congo said.

He arrived early at the Elysian Hotel, bought a *Wall Street Journal* from the lobby concession and found a gondola chair at the base of the escalator where no one could pass up to the Grand Ballroom and the meeting without him seeing.

Rachel Lee Krebs came in from the forecourt and rode up. Intent on whatever business had brought her, she looked straight ahead and didn't appear to notice him. Pat Easter arrived shortly afterward.

"John, I'm glad you've had a change of heart." He backed up the statement with an enthusiastic handclasp.

"Do you have a minute to chat before the meeting starts?" Congo inquired.

"Of course."

The two men retreated into the depths of the huge lobby, well away from the escalators and the traffic flow, where art deco sofas made a conversation square before a marble fireplace.

"First," Congo said after they had seated themselves. "I want to thank you for convincing the police that Raymond's death was an accident. Of course, I realize

Hillman was abusing Rachel, so he couldn't have her talking out of school, but you still kept me out of a tough spot."

Easter's smile fidgeted. "The police shared Rachel's statement with you?"

"They had to complete their report. I was one of the last people to see Raymond alive."

The two statements were true on their face, but potentially false in their implication. Congo's expression betrayed no hint of fraud, Easter's no shortage of skepticism.

"Then you know," Easter said, "that Stepanian was on his way to confront you when Rachel tried to get the gun away from him."

Congo shook his head. "Raymond was murdered. Shot without warning and with no chance to defend himself."

The small muscles in Easter's face tightened but he held his tongue.

"Raymond wasn't the type for confrontation," Congo explained. "When he got in over his head, he ran to Uncle Gregory. He had no gun when I threw him out of the hotel. He probably kept one in his car only as a last resort."

"Rachel's statement—"

"Rachel came to see me the day after," Congo pushed on. "She pointed a .22 at me and accused me of killing Raymond."

"She is a disturbed young woman," Easter said.

"If she were a true split personality, neither Rachel nor Lee would be consciously aware that the other existed."

"Rachel fired the fatal shot," Easter insisted. "Forensic evidence proved that to police satisfaction."

"Rachel killed Raymond the man," Congo corrected. "She was accusing me of killing Raymond the dream."

Easter stared in confusion.

"To you and me," Congo said, "Raymond was a loser. But to Rachel, he had possibilities. She could finally have a stalwart hubby, just like the pretty girls did. As long as she was part of the Elysian Hotel package, Raymond was willing to tease her along. When I threw him out, he told her to get lost. Her bubble burst and her self control went with it. She probably dropped the gun after she shot him. He picked it up and made his way to the lobby to find help."

Congo glanced at the front door where Raymond had collapsed. As if on cue, Stu Forrest walked in looking every inch the Elysian's largest shareholder in a navy blue blazer and sharply pressed gray slacks. He wore no tie and had foregone his morning shave. He saw Congo and Easter and started over.

Easter paled.

"Relax," Congo said. "I'm not criticizing your solution. Raymond was no loss. Even if he was, nothing will bring him back. Rachel is the only one left to save, and maybe she can be turned around by counseling. That is the deal, isn't it? Raymond died accidentally and Rachel agrees to undergo treatment?"

"Yes," Easter admitted. "It is."

"By the way," Congo said as the two of them stood, "my attorney got a call from the police wondering if I knew where Gregory Demirjian had gotten off to."

"According to information Royce received informally," Easter said, "the police are now satisfied that Mr. Demirjian is no longer in the country."

Forrest arrived with a wink at Congo. "I knew you'd find your way to the winning side before the actual vote," he said, adding, "you won't regret it," as they shook hands.

Congo just smiled.

Forrest shook hands with Easter. "I think I saw Royce pull up outside."

A Town Car was visible through the front glass of the lobby. Royce Hillman held a rear door for Karen Steele. She came out with a buoyant toss of her hair and an effervescent smile.

Forrest said, "Let's button-hole Royce before he goes up to the meeting. Get him to call the vote in order of number of shares held. If the four large holdings vote yes, the others will fall in line. A unanimous vote will give us a hot hand going into the next round of negotiations."

"I was just about to suggest that to John," Easter said as they set off to intercept Hillman at the main door.

Congo wasn't paying attention. "Pat," he said, "do you think it's a good idea having Rachel work the shareholder's meeting?"

"Excuse me?"

"Raymond died here in the hotel. This place almost certainly has unpleasant associations for her."

"Rachel is out sick today."

"I don't think so. Unless she really is twin sisters, that's her coming down the escalator."

It was mid morning and there were few riders on the moving staircase. Rachel was the only passenger coming down. The escalator wasn't fast enough for her. She walked as well. Her posture was erect, her jaw set. She had one hand inside the denim bag slung from her shoulder.

Near the base of the escalator a proximity mechanism opened the main lobby door. Hillman and Karen passed through, engrossed in conversation. The door closed behind them. Rachel took the .22 target automatic out of her bag and brought it up in both hands.

Easter's shouted warning dissolved into the pop of gunfire. The pistol cycled as rapidly as Rachel could pull the trigger, flashing at the muzzle and springing spent casings from the ejection port.

Karen screamed and jumped aside, losing her balance in three inch heels and going down.

Terror filled Hillman's moon face. He backpedaled until he collided with the door. Several rounds starred the laminated glass around him. At least one found its target. Hillman slid down the glass to a sitting position.

Rachel's pistol locked open, empty.

The whole thing took only seconds; not enough time to send bystanders scrambling for cover. Two men caught Rachel at the base of the escalator and tried to wrestle the automatic away from her. She fought savagely, screaming and kicking, still trying to fire the empty weapon into Hillman.

Arterial blood pulsed from Hillman's throat. It dribbled like soup down his collar to stain the front of his shirt. His mouth moved but he couldn't manage words.

"911!" Easter yelled. "Call 911!"

The concierge was already on the phone.

Karen scrambled to her feet and knelt beside Hillman, calling his name without getting his attention. Easter knelt on the other side and together they pulled his shoulders away from the glass to get him into a more comfortable position. As soon as his weight was gone, the proximity mechanism took over and retracted the glass. Hillman's torso was too heavy and clumsily positioned for them to manage and he sagged backward to leave him laying half inside and half outside.

A siren emitted an intersection-clearing burst, drawing attention to a fire department medical truck in traffic. Congo stepped behind Karen and took her shoulders in his hands.

"Nothing you can do," he said gently and tried to draw her back from Hillman.

Her head snapped around and she glared wordlessly.

"Come on, Karen," Congo said. "You have to give the paramedics room to work."

She stood, shaking her shoulders free. The fire department van pulled up outside with its strobes flashing. Two EMTs piled out and retrieved armloads of impact cases from the back. Congo and Karen stepped back from Hillman to make way for them.

Rachel sat sobbing on the floor with her face buried in her hands. Two men stood close to her. One held her empty pistol. Neither seemed quite sure what he should do.

"Who is she?" Karen asked.

"She had plans for Gregory Demirjian's nephew," Congo said. "Hillman destroyed her dream. I guess she decided to destroy his. Maybe Demirjian put a bug in her ear about it. Maybe she thought it up on her own. I don't know."

The police arrived and began sorting witnesses from gawkers. Rachel was taken away. An ambulance came. Hillman was loaded carefully onto a gurney. Forrest joined Karen and Congo as they moved back to give the police room to string yellow tape.

"Tough break," Forrest said. "We were a heartbeat away from sewing up the Athens deal.

Karen managed a smile. "We will. We'll have to postpone the meeting, of course, but when Royce—"

Forrest shook his head. "Royce isn't going to make it. Not from the way the paramedics were talking."

Karen's eyes widened.

"Hillman Management was the operating cornerstone of Athens," Forrest said. "It will probably have to be sold off to pay the estate taxes."

Karen swayed and her face lost color. Congo helped her to a nearby sofa and sat beside her. Forrest, who was personally acquainted with the other Elysian owners volunteered to help Easter call the people in the Grand Ballroom to cancel the shareholders' vote. Karen watched him press a Bluetooth into his ear and begin talking.

"It's all just so stupid," she said.

"Chaos theory," Congo said.

"What?"

"A butterfly flaps its wings in China and sets off a chain reaction that blows a hurricane into the Caribbean."

She gave him a look. "You don't believe that."

"A week ago I came within two inches of what happened to Hillman. There was a reason for it, locked up and buried in some obscure chain of events, but none of us involved will ever know what it was."

"So what should we do?" she asked. "Surrender to fate?"

"That's not what I'm saying. I came to L.A. chasing a dream. It's turning out to be a lot tougher than I expected, mostly as a result of things I didn't know and couldn't have predicted. I think you've just collided with the same thing."

She offered no argument. He put an arm on the back of the sofa, behind her shoulders.

"Since we're both in the same situation, we might be good candidates to help each other over the rough spots. Even if it's only aid and comfort to start with."

"You're certainly persistent."

"Committed," he corrected.

"And if I say no?"

"Then I hope we can still do business. I do need your help leasing the Crestline vacancies."

She lapsed into thought and when she made eye contact again her natural buoyancy had been replaced by solemn concern.

"I have to hear you say you're serious. That this isn't just something you're doing for the thrill of the chase."

"I couldn't be more serious," he confessed.

She settled against him. "You have no idea what you're getting into."

END

978-0-595-43853-2
0-595-43853-9